A. H. HAGA

Survival Kit

First published by Haga Books 2021

First edition

Cover art by Ravven

*This book was professionally typeset on Reedsy.
Find out more at reedsy.com*

To the Millions Missing.

Contents

Preface

Myalgic Encephalomyelitis is a neurological condition that affects the whole body. No M.E.-patient has precisely the same experience of the disease. Some have mild symptoms and can work. Others spend their lives in bed in a dark room, too weak and hurting even to eat.

This book is based on my own experience with the condition.

I was diagnosed in 2014 after years of symptoms, and have steadily gotten worse. I now have Severe Myalgic Encephalomyelitis, meaning I am mostly homebound, if not bedbound, and move around with the help of a wheelchair.

Therefore, this book is extremely personal to me, and I am giving you a snapshot of what it is to live in my body, as I couldn't fit all of my symptoms into Kit or this world.

I am not a spokesperson for disabled, wheelchair-users, or M.E.-patients. This book is not a medical text or the answer to what it is like for everyone to have M.E.

Thank you so much for reading.

1

I t took all of a month for the world to end, and it felt like we were the only ones left. I didn't want it to be true, but I hadn't gotten any proof otherwise.

"How does it look out there?" Shadia asked as she entered the living room and placed a rucksack by my feet.

"All empty," I answered as I bent and picked it up. I didn't bother looking through it, knowing it would contain medication, food, water, and blankets. The things we deemed most important. We'd talked it over many times, and I trusted her.

"You ready, then?" Shadia continued, making sure her rucksack sat secure. She was dressed in hiking boots, shorts, and a t-shirt. A jacket hung tied around her waist, the bottom half of her shorts lay in one of the thigh pockets–the pants had a zipper at the knee–and she had a knife hung at her belt. A pair of bright pink gloves shone against her golden-brown skin. Her dark, curly hair was drawn back from her face into a ponytail so it wouldn't get in the way.

"Guess so," I answered and lifted the rucksack, slipping its straps over the handles of my chair.

Shadia narrowed her eyes at me. "We could stay one more day, but I don't think it would make any difference."

I looked away. "I know, I know. I just don't want to, that's all. You sure you shouldn't go without me? I'll only slow you down and–"

She cut me off. "Stop it. We've talked about this. I'm not going without you, no matter what."

"But you know I'm right!" I barked back. "You know bringing me will most likely get us both killed."

"And I might as well die if I don't bring you!" she yelled back before closing her eyes and drawing a deep breath.

I knew she meant it, and that left me between a rock and a hard place. If she stayed, we would probably die. If she brought me, I might slow her down and we might die. That 'might' was what decided it for me in the end.

Calmed, Shadia walked over and sank down in front of me, taking my hands, resting them within her own in my lap. "I know you're scared. I'm scared too, but we can do this. We get out of town today and find a car tomorrow. With a car, we should be there by tomorrow night, right?" I nodded. "So, let's do this."

"But what if we can't find a car? Or what if the streets are clogged all the way to Vestfold og Telemark? What if we run into them? What if they're already on the island?"

"Don't worry about those things. I'll deal with that. As long as you're with me, I know I can do this."

She kissed my hands and looked up at me, her brown eyes big and pleading. I stared into them, wanting to drown in them and forget everything else except the two of us, but the unnatural silence that hung outside the windows was an eerie reminder of the state of the world, and I looked away. I didn't mind staying behind and dying, but no way was I going to let Shadia die because of me. No way.

2

"Fine," I sighed. "Let's go."

She grinned and shot up to kiss me. As she was moving to stand, I grabbed the strap of her rucksack and pulled her back to me. I kissed the tip of her nose. She leaned down and did the same, resting her forehead against mine for a second before pulling back.

"You have everything?" she asked, her eyes roaming over me.

"Yeah." I pointed to the messenger bag standing against the wall by my feet. As I reached for it, she grabbed it and slung it over her shoulder. "Won't that be too heavy for you?" I scowled.

"Nah, I'm mostly carrying clothes. You got all the heavy stuff."

I wanted to point out it would be heavy for her too, but rolled my eyes instead and leaned down to make sure my Doc Marten's were tied properly. They were summer boots and fitted well, but I had winter boots in the messenger bag. We'd talked about bringing more clothes, but most of the heavy winter-gear was already at the cabin, and bringing more would only slow us down.

Shadia's family had celebrated Christmas at the island cabin for her entire life, and I'd spent a few holidays there myself. Few used the area in winter, so we felt like we were the only people in the world. Not unlike now. I shuddered and pushed the thought away.

Compared to Shadia, I didn't look ready for the trek at all. I was wearing black jeans and the Docs, and a black tank top with my leather jacket slung over the top. On my head sat a wide-brimmed hat that almost hid my dyed green pixie cut. My face was pale from years spent mostly inside, and I wore sunglasses even now. The only color I wore was the pink bike gloves on my hands, matching Shadia's. They were a gift from her a few years back.

We'd argued about what I should wear for this trip, but I didn't have any workout clothes anymore. She'd said she could lend me some, but I declined. Her clothes were too large to fit me, and their fabric would irritate my skin anyway. There were many things to think about for a trip like this to succeed, even without considering my fucked up body.

With a last sigh, I pushed a piece of gum into my mouth and unlocked the brakes on my wheelchair. "Let's go."

Shadia gave a nod and walked to stand behind me, gripping the handles and maneuvering me away from the wall.

I threw one last glance out the window, but the street was as quiet now as it had been before our little spat.

I'd seen a few of them over the last few days as they moved past the cars and houses, and I'd been afraid they would come for us, but somehow they hadn't noticed us up on the fourth floor.

Shadia opened the front door and pushed me out before turning and locking it behind us. The thought of locking a door when we were the only living people we'd seen in weeks made me want to cackle with panic, but I kept it in. Instead, I considered teasing Shadia about doing it, but the act was so natural that it felt wrong to mention it.

We kept silent as she wheeled me down the hallway. When we reached the elevator, she stopped and mumbled something I didn't catch. I turned to look up at her, taking off my sunglasses to see in the dim hall. The power had gone out days ago, which was when we started talking about going to the cabin. Neither of us had thought about the elevator not working, though.

"What now?" I asked.

She sighed. "I guess we take the stairs."

"How?

"One at a time."

She glowered and wheeled me toward the door leading to the stairs. Pushing it open with her butt, she wheeled me in backwards. The door closed with a metal bang, plunging us into darkness.

2

The trip down the stairs was a mess. While Shadia was prepared for dark places and had brought headlamps and regular flashlights, she hadn't been prepared for stairs and a wheelchair.

I couldn't help thinking that this was a bad sign, as I was sure we would have to run at some point, maybe into a building and up stairs, but I didn't voice my thoughts. Right now, I was trying to stay positive and help Shadia as much as I could, even if it felt like she was jolting my spleen out my mouth with every step, and I almost swallowed my piece of gum at the same time. It was not pleasant.

"You should've just carried me down first," I said in-between groans.

"Shut up," she answered in a puff, pushing her butt back to hit me in the back of the head. "I've got this."

I didn't answer but rolled my eyes and scanned the dark stairwell. There were no signs of any struggle; no blood on the walls, and no bodies on the stairs. The only sign people had left in a panic was the forgotten teddy bear on the second-floor landing. I pictured Jimmy from the apartment across from us, hugging the bear tight as his father carried him down the stairs. Someone must have bumped into them, and Jimmy lost his grip. When he cried out for his lost friend, his father didn't dare turn back to look for it, carried with the flow of people as they were, and the teddy was forgotten.

Not that I was sure the teddy had belonged to Jimmy. For all I knew he didn't have any stuffed bears, but he was the only kid I knew in the building.

Shadia bumped my head with her ass again and muttered in Arabic as she straightened.

"We down?" I asked and reached for the wheels. I was pretty sure I'd kept up with the floors, but between all the bumping and Shadia's mumbling, I might have messed up the count.

"We are down," Shadia answered, and I turned around.

She was stretching her back before trying to loosen up her shoulders. I watched her limber up for a moment before I rolled to the door. She didn't stop me before the palm of my hand, protected by the glove, was on the handle.

"Maybe I should check the lobby is empty first?" she said.

I turned to look at her, my headlamp making her squint. "I'm sure we would've heard them if they were in the lobby," I answered flatly and pushed on the handle, still only touching it with my gloved palm.

Shadia jumped forward, ready to grab and pull me back, but the door opened to an empty lobby. The late summer light shone through the big glass doors at the front of the building. Nothing moved anywhere in sight.

"See?" I said and rolled out, turning off my headlamp and pulling down my sunglasses again as I waited for her to close the door behind us. Shadia grabbed my handles before I rolled another meter. She didn't stop me as I feared she would, but pushed me forward. I considered arguing that I could move on my own, but I also knew we would move faster this way, so I kept my mouth shut.

Through the glass in the front door, I could see an empty street. Cars stood along the other side of the road, and other than some trash lying forgotten on the asphalt, it was completely still.

"What's the plan if we meet any of them?" I asked as I reached forward and unlocked the front door, using bent fingers so only my joints touched the metal.

The moment I opened the door, I was hit with a smell so bitter I almost gagged. Instantly, I could taste the death on the air, and I spat out my gum into the lobby.

"Ew!" Shadia exclaimed, stepping aside so as not to be hit by the wad of gum. "You could have spit it outside."

"You know birds might get stuck in it," I answered as I grimaced against the smell.

Shadia didn't answer before the door had clicked shut behind us. Looking up at her, I saw she was blinking against the sharp light, looking up and down the street. Looking for cars or them, I wasn't sure which.

"Back to the original question; run and hide," she answered when she was sure we were alone, and started pushing me up the street.

"Where're we going? The station's that way." I pointed over my shoulder, twisting to look up at her again.

"Keep your eyes straight ahead and tell me if you see anyone, OK?" she said and glanced down at me. When I didn't turn, she leaned down and placed a quick kiss on my forehead. I mumbled my agreement and turned forward, squinting to try and see better. "The station might have closed down when things started going South, but it's in the middle of town, and that's where people gathered, so I'm sure there's still a bunch of them there. I want to try and avoid the most crowded places."

That made sense.

"So going for Ring Three?" Oslo was split into rings. Ring One was at the center, where we lived, and the most crowded, with the shopping street of Karl Johan, the royal castle, hotels, and the main train station. Ring Two was less crowded, and Ring Three the least so. The freeway ran through all of them, but I was sure Shadia was right, and the streets within Ring One would be clogged with both cars and people.

"Yeah, I think that might be best. Get to Ring Three and onto the freeway from there. Find a car and drive all the way to Borøya. Sounds like a plan to you?"

"Yeah, guess so."

We rolled on in silence for a while.

We'd left our street behind, and I couldn't help looking around. I hadn't left the apartment for over a year now. After my legs stopped working, it felt like more of a hassle than it was worth to go out, so I only left when going to the doctors or other errands I had to do. That meant I got into our car and was driven to wherever I was going by Shadia or someone else willing to help, and I didn't bother looking around. Now, out in the bright light of the August sun and with the world quiet around me, I took it all in, wondering for a moment why I had shut myself away in the first place.

Something clattered up ahead, and Shadia stopped. We stood still for half a minute, listening. It might just be a dog left to its own devices after its owners died, or one of the many stray cats or rats that had roamed the city before things went to shit. But it could also be something much worse.

During that half-minute, the clattering came twice more, seeming to always come from the same place and distance.

When it didn't come any closer, I glanced up at Shadia, who looked back down at me. Without a word, I gave a little nod, and she pushed me forward.

As we neared Bislett Stadium–a big, white oval used for all the sporting events one could think of–the clattering grew louder and faster. Like if a wind had picked up and was snapping a flag, but there was no wind right now. It would have blown my hat right off.

Our progress almost slowed to a crawl; we came into view of the many doors leading into the stadium.

Shadia jerked to a halt and gasped. I was speechless as I stared at the glass doors and the people pressed against them. They stood packed, women and children and men dressed in regular clothing. There hadn't been any sporting events, but I knew that the stadium had been used as a refugee center for people from evacuated buildings.

Still barely breathing, I grabbed the wheels and drew myself out of Shadia's grip.

"Kit," she hissed, "what are you doing?"

"I just wanna take a look," I answered, not taking my eyes off the people.

"Come back here!" Her voice was barely audible over the noise from the doors. As close as I was, I saw what had made the clattering sound. One of the windows was loose and kept almost falling out of its frame whenever the people on the inside pulled back, and was pushed back against the metal frame when they surged forward again, trying to get out.

Just a meter away from the doors now, I looked up at the people inside. Their eyes were trained on me as they scraped their nails and teeth against the glass, trying to break it without knowing how. Their skin was grey and dead; on some, it had started to rot, and all of them were oozing something. The woman right in front of me was missing an eye, the skin around the empty socket ripped to pieces by what I guess must have been a bird of some kind. Maggots filled the socket, wiggling and crawling. I felt my stomach move and want to empty, but I swallowed the bile. The woman's other eye was trained on me; the pupil dilated until it filled her whole iris, making whatever color it had been disappear, replaced by all black.

"Katerina Ingunn Tanum, get back here!" Shadia hissed, her voice making me jump and push the chair forward.

We'd filled the wheels with new air before leaving, so the chair was a lot more movable than before. I was unused to it, and this movability made the chair roll straight into the door.

The thud I made was small, but the people on the other side surged forward as a wave. The glass pane that had been falling inward was pushed back into the metal frame with a loud slam that made me grit my teeth.

A crack formed in the glass on impact.

I sat, frozen, as the crack spread with surprising speed until it spider-webbed across the entire window. The woman with only one eye was pushed against the door by the people behind, and her teeth snagging on one of the cracks. I heard a click as her teeth touched the glass, then the whole thing splintered, looking like a fog for half a heartbeat before falling away. Nothing was left between the woman and me as she fell over the middle bar of the door. Other zombies leaned over her, arms stretching toward me.

3

I screamed and used my legs to push away from the door. They may not carry me, but at that moment, I thanked whoever wanted to listen that they still worked. Pain flared up my legs as I placed them back onto the foot-holds, but I gritted my teeth and ignored it as best I could.

"I told you not to go closer!" Shadia bellowed as she grabbed my handles and spun me around.

I just had time to see the first zombie claw its way over the middle bar of the door and thump onto the asphalt before I was facing the street again. Shadia was running, pushing me with all she was worth.

Turning in my chair, I looked back to see the first zombie getting to its legs and stumbling after us. Others were following through the opening, falling on top of each other.

I was about to turn back around, breathing a sigh of relief, when a wet sound reached me, and I saw the torso of the woman with one missing eye thump to the ground. Black blood oozed from her midriff as she lifted her head and focused that one eye on me.

"What was that?" Shadia yelled, panic making her voice high and warbled.

I spun back around in my seat, covering my mouth, trying

not to throw up. Holy crap, had I just seen that? Tears filled my eyes, and I lifted my glasses, hurriedly drying them away. Why was I crying?

We reached the top of the street, and Shadia stopped running. When I looked up, I saw she was turned around, looking back the way we'd come. I saw her dark eyes focus on the people making their way up the street toward us, shambling and seeming unsure of their own bodies. Thankfully, they were slow.

I let out a breath of relief and turned back around, looking at the round-about before us, wondering where to go next. In front of us, the street was clogged with cars, some even parked up on the sidewalk that we would have to weave around, but she wasn't looking at that.

My mind froze as something moved between the many cars, and it took three full heartbeats before I could think again. "Uhm, Sha?" I said, not taking my eyes off the movements.

"What?" Shadia asked. I could hear by her voice that she was still turned away.

"I think we should move."

"Why? They're not that fast. I think we're safe for now."

"No, we're not."

"Why?"

I turned around and slapped her hip. "Just look!"

She glared down at me for half a second before she followed my pointed finger with her eyes. Her jaw clenched and her eyes grew wide, fear making her pupils grow large for a second.

The cars were packed nose to bumper, but in the little room between them stood zombies. They lay over the hoods of the cars or the roofs, clawing at the shining paint to get at us. Two of the cars had zombies inside them, clawing and biting at the windows to get out. Moaning and clacking filled the air until my head was buzzing. The sounds seemed to come from all over. Why hadn't I noticed before? Or had I, but it was drowned out by the rushing of blood as I looked at the zombies inside the stadium?

As we stood, frozen and watching, one of the zombies managed to drag its lower body onto the hood of a car and crawl over it, falling face-first onto the pavement but pushing up before its feet hit the ground.

Shadia cursed in Arabic.

"I think we should move now," I managed, not taking my eyes off the zombie as it stood. It had been a man, once, probably handsome if I was to guess from the sandy hair and the broad shoulders.

"Yes," Shadia agreed.

A shudder ran through my chair as she grabbed the handles and pushed me around.

Glancing back the way we had come, I saw that the zombies from the stadium had gotten dangerously close. If we didn't hurry, they would catch up to us.

"We gotta go," I murmured.

Shadia didn't need to be told twice. She started jogging, pushing me in front, and we rattled over the tram tracks.

My eyes, jumping around and trying to focus on everything at once, found an opening between the cars on the round-about up ahead, two zombies having already got through it.

"Sha ..." I began.

"I see them," she growled.

"What do we do? There's nowhere to go!" I wasn't joking. On our left side were buildings and fences. On our right was the round-about and its moat of cars and dead people. Behind

14

were dead people, and in front were dead people.

"We have to go through," Shadia said.

I spun to look up at her, the chair twisting with the sudden movement. "What?"

Without another word, she let go of my chair with one hand. With my weight all messed up from being turned around, my chair wobbled and almost tipped, but she was able to keep me straight, never taking her eyes of the zombies ahead. We were rushing at them, and they would be upon us in two steps. With her free hand, she grabbed the knife at her belt and pulled it loose from its sheath. Before I could ask what she was doing, she almost threw it in my face. I reached up on instinct and took it. Before I had a proper grip, she was holding my chair with both hands again and was bowling me into one of the zombies.

I screamed as my feet hit its shins, making it topple toward my face. I reached up and grabbed it by the shoulders, flipping it to the side. Before it even hit the asphalt, we were past, Shadia running full out. My hat almost flew off my head, but I was able to grab at it and keep it in place.

We left the second zombie behind, but there was no time to celebrate as more of them were flowing from between the cars. Shadia did what she could to avoid them, pushing me up as close as she could to the fence on our left, but they were still coming.

Not thinking about the pain it may cause, I turned in my chair, flinging one leg over the armrest and kicking out. I hit the zombie that had been coming at us in the chest and threw it back into two others, making them all fall over.

I couldn't help the sound of mixed pain and joy escaping me before I turned forward again, making sure none of them got in our way.

Finally, we reached the next street. My own eyes hadn't even properly focused on it before Shadia sighed and pushed me down it. It was empty, thankfully.

Shadia didn't stop running, and when I was sure no dead people would jump us from the front, I turned and looked back. We were four cars down the street, and already the entrance was clogged with the walking dead.

She let go of one handle to squeeze my shoulder once. I leaned into her hand, focusing on the love in it and not the mild burn of the pressure.

Careful not to mess with our speed and balance, I reached back, pushing my hand between the rucksack and the back of the chair, and into the pockets there. I pulled out the cola bottle we'd stashed there before finding my pillbox in the pocket of my jacket. I was starting to sweat, a hot flash coming on, but I didn't have the energy to take my jacket off. My hands were shaking as I pulled off the gloves and used an anti-bacterial wipe to clean my hands. Skin still smelling of alcohol, the scent almost overpowering, I opened the box and picked up a small yellow and green capsule. I popped it in my mouth before I unscrewed the coke and swallowed the pain-pill with two gulps.

After screwing on the lid, I kept the coke between my legs, within easy reach, and pulled on my gloves again.

"Close your eyes and rest until it kicks in," Shadia said. "We're safe for now."

I didn't quite believe her, but I closed my eyes anyway. The sound of my wheels across the asphalt and Shadia's breathing almost drowned out the sound of moaning and bodies falling against cars behind us. Almost.

16

4

I sat on the sofa at home with my legs pulled up under me and stared at the letter. I couldn't feel the hands holding it, and a headache was hammering behind my eyes. I swore that was the reason I was crying, not the words.

I sat like that, not moving, for almost an hour before Shadia came home, her hair still wet from the showers at the gym.

"Hey, habibi!" she called before she disappeared into the bathroom as she always did the moment she got home. I was pretty sure she didn't use it, just took a few moments to herself to prepare to meet me. She never knew what she would come home to, after all.

Today had been a good day. I'd been able to empty the dishwasher. At least it would be one thing less for her to worry about.

She exited the bathroom after half an hour. I still hadn't been able to look up, but my eyes jumped when I saw her shadow on the floor.

"What's that?" she asked and fell onto the sofa beside me.

I handed her the letter, my joints creaking from lack of use. It felt like I was a puppet forgotten in storage for a long time. A puppet with wormholes in the head and legs filled with pain, but no one saw the pain on the puppet's painted face.

"Are you kidding me?" Shadia almost screamed the words. "They *can't do this! This time, we get a lawyer. I don't care what you say, I'm calling them tomorrow."*

"Why bother?" I asked, my voice low and hoarse from the tears I was trying to hold at bay.

Shadia moved to me and took my face in both hands. They were warm and felt unreal against my skin. "Kit, habibi, you have a right. You got sick, and the treatment made you even sicker. It isn't your fault you're the way you are."

"They don't believe me."

"No, one person doesn't believe you. Your caseworker believes you, I believe you, our friends and family believe you."

"But what if they're right? What if it's all really in my head?"

"Did the shrink say that when you were there last year?" I shook my head. "No, because this isn't in your head. This is a neurological disease that is slowly eating you up, and I won't let one asshole at NAV try to convince you otherwise. We will find a lawyer, and we will send a complaint, you hear me?" I nodded. "Good."

She let my face go and crumpled the letter into a small ball before tossing it toward the other side of the room. When she turned to me again, she was smiling, and the smile moved from her lips to mine as they touched, even if it didn't quite reach my eyes.

On the other side of the room, the letter unfolded a little, the words 'Request for disability income: denied' barely visible.

Shadia's hand on my shoulder brought me out of the hot daze. I had to shake my head a couple of times to dislodge the memory, wondering why I'd thought of that now. It's not like NAV was a problem anymore.

It took me a moment to realize we weren't moving.

"Why did we stop?" I asked and looked around. We stood in front of a hotel. The glass doors at the top of the steps were broken, but otherwise, it looked untouched.

"I thought maybe we should stop for the day," Shadia said, her voice light. It was the tone she used when she wanted me to make a decision about my health but didn't quite trust me to make the right one.

"No," I said, knowing it was the answer she expected and dreaded. I turned to look at her, having to tilt my hat back to do so. "We're not even close to out of the city. We need to keep going."

She looked at my face, trying to meet my eyes through the glasses. "Kit, you fell asleep in the chair. You shouldn't push yourself."

"You know I've already done that. If we stop now … I'm afraid I won't get started again." Her jaw tightened, and the worry in her eyes almost cut me. "So if you're asking me, I think we should keep going a little longer. We need to get as far as we can today, and stopping now won't help anyone."

Shadia worked her jaw a couple of times before she looked away. "OK. If you're sure."

"I am." She didn't move, and I knew she was considering to argue. It was an argument we'd had many times, and I usually listened to her. It wouldn't be the first time I wasn't thinking clearly because of adrenaline or because I was tired. But I couldn't let her win this time. It wasn't just about my health anymore. It was about her life. "But considering we've already stopped," I said, and she looked at me, hope in her eyes, "I think you should go in."

"Me?"

"Yeah. We only have your knife for a weapon, and while it works, it's clear I need to be able to defend myself as well. My legs won't always work," I said, smiling.

She didn't return my smile. "And where would I find a weapon in a hotel?"

I shrugged. "Fire axes? They might have those hanging around. Or butcher's knives from the kitchen."

Shadia looked up at the hotel with narrowed eyes. Finally, she looked around. The street was empty, even if the smell of rotten flesh clung to us.

"I'll use the time to rest," I said. "Just roll me into the shadows, and I'll be fine."

It took almost a minute before Shadia finally nodded. I kept from giving myself a high five for having convinced her and sat demurely as she rolled me into the shadows. She turned my chair, so I had my back to the wall and the stairs leading into the hotel on my other side. A modicum of protection. Then, she pulled the knife from its sheath and held it out to me.

"Nope," I said. "You take it. What if someone's holed up in that hotel and doesn't want to share the space? Or the weapons?"

Shadia rolled her eyes. "You watch too many of those dystopian shows." She grabbed my hand and wrapped it around the hilt. Before I could let go, she stepped back, leaving me with the knife. "If any of them come, you need that more than me."

"There might be zombies in the hotel," I argued.

"The hotels were closed down. No one would have died in there."

"Why're the doors broken, then?"

"Probably looters."

"Exactly! And they might still be in there."

Shadia glowered. I looked away, lowering my hand with the

knife into my lap.

"Fine," I grumbled, which actually made Shadia smile.

"Rest well. I'll be right back."

"Be careful!"

"Always am."

She rounded the stairs and hurried up them. I heard her step on glass before silence. Even so, I strained to listen. How long would it take her to find axes? They were on every floor, right?

Forcing myself to relax, I drank the rest of my cola and leaned my head back against the wall. My chair had a higher back than most everyday wheelchairs because I needed the support and a slight tip to keep dizziness at bay, but there was nowhere to rest my head. It was the one thing I missed when I got tired, but having a higher back would make the chair even more unruly, and having a light chair that I could move around in was more important than somewhere to rest my head. Most times, I had a bed or sofa for that anyway.

Time ticked by, and I'd almost slipped back into a doze when a sound reached me. I rubbed my dry eyes and looked around. Hand still over one eye, I froze. Two figures were walking up the sidewalk, heading straight for me.

It took me a second to focus my tired eyes, and when I did, I almost wished I hadn't. There was no doubt they were zombies. They had once been a man and a woman, and they were dressed in matching pajama-sets. The woman had one slipper on, her other foot naked and crusted in dried blood. Blood soaked the front of their shirts and ran down from between their legs, making the fabric stick to their skin. Other than that, they looked almost alive. Really pale, but alive. They couldn't have been dead long.

"Shadia?" I called. She must be close by, right? She'd been in there for a while, and it wouldn't take that long to find axes. But only the zombies answered, seeming to increase their speed at the sound of my voice.

My hands trembling, I reached down to undo the brakes but thought better of it. In this corner, I was partly protected. If more of the zombies were coming from the other side, leaving the corner would place me right between them, exposed and surrounded. But what if these two came any closer? Should I try to avoid them?

The zombies didn't give me a chance to decide. The man was a little faster than the woman, and he was almost speed-walking now. It looked weird, his legs dragging, and arms flapping like he didn't know how to use them.

My hands found the knife in my lap, and I lifted it. "Stay back!" I called, feeling silly the moment the words left my mouth. The zombies wouldn't understand me.

The man didn't stop. Instead, he mimicked my motion and lifted his arms, reaching for me.

I slashed, and the knife bit into his palm. It was almost jerked from my hand by the change of momentum. The zombie only continued forward. I screamed as he reached for my face, sluggish blood oozing from his hand. My feet went up and I kicked him between the legs. He didn't react, but the movement put him off balance, and he all but fell into my lap, head over the armrest.

Still screaming, I slammed the knife into his back again and again, but he continued moving.

A small part of my mind hollered to go for the head. The only way to kill a zombie was by ruining the head, after all, but my body wouldn't listen.

As the woman reached us, I moved my knees up, pushing the man off me in the same motion. He stumbled back, leaving a trail of black blood as he went. Kicking out with one foot, I pushed him further away.

The woman walked right past him and bent, her mouth open and showing bloody teeth. I pushed the knife forward and it slipped into her open mouth and up past her throat. Her teeth scraped across my glove, but I hardly felt it.

My grip on the handle was slick, and I almost lost the knife as the woman went suddenly limp, but I managed to jerk it out at the last second.

The man had fallen at my kick and was crawling toward me now. It made his head easier to reach, and I slammed the knife down just as he reached for my leg.

This time, when he fell, I let the knife fall with him.

I stared at the two zombies for a moment before looking at my hands. They were covered in the dark, almost dry blood, but my gloves were fine. There was no visible rip or tear, and I didn't feel the sting of a wound.

Hands shaking, I looked over the rest of me. There were flecks of the dark blood on my jeans and jacket, but not the bloodbath I'd expected. How many times had I stabbed the man? At least five, but he'd hardly bled.

My sight grew blurry, and I almost dried away the tears, but I didn't dare touch the blood to my bare skin. What if whatever made a zombie transmitted through blood, and I got it in my eyes? Would that be enough? Or the saliva of the woman that must be on my fingers, even if I couldn't see it?

I realized I was still screaming, and had been screaming through the entire fight. I clicked my teeth shut so hard it hurt.

That's how Shadia found me a few seconds later: my mouth jammed shut against the noises inside, my hands out in front of me, covered in dark blood and shaking, tears streaming down my face.

She stopped, taking in the scene, and she turn almost as white as those zombies I'd killed. I didn't know Shadia could get that pale, and I didn't like it. I preferred her warm golden skin. The thought was so random it almost made me laugh. I kept my mouth shut, keeping that in as well, but at least it ruined the scream that was stuck in my throat.

I let out a breath and finally looked up at Shadia. "See?" I said, voice barely shaking. "I said I could take care of myself." Shadia only stared. "Any chance you found any towels?" I asked. "I would really like to clean this off."

This made Shadia move. She took a couple of steps forward, dropped the two axes she was carrying, and stopped over me, looking down at the two zombies. Then she began to laugh. It was a tad too bright and loud, but I didn't interrupt her. Just let her laugh it out.

When she was done, she turned and rested her head atop mine. I couldn't see her face or even her neck because of the brim of my hat, but the contact calmed me and did the same for her. We stood like that for a long moment before she pulled back.

"Give me a second, *habibi;* there was a bathroom in the lobby."

I nodded and watched as she walked away, strangely calm. It was then I realized why I'd had that dream about NAV and my denied request. I had felt so helpless at that moment, like I could do nothing right, and that was how I felt after our first run-in with the undead. Now, however, I had proven that I could kill them on my own. It might have been sloppy and messy, but I'd killed them both on my own. That feeling of helplessness no longer lay in my stomach like a rock.

The thought that something good had come out of this encounter almost made me laugh as well, but I kept it down. In doing so, I felt a bit more control return to my mind. I wasn't helpless, and I could do this. I could keep Shadia alive long enough for us to get to Borøya. To get us to our safe haven.

5

I washed my hands with towels and water three times, then used antibacterial-gel on both my gloves and my skin. Finally, I let Shadia inspect my hands for any rifts or tears, but there was nothing there. I'd been lucky.

Adrenaline was still prickling under my skin when I pulled on my gloves, and we were ready to go. Shadia wanted to stay in the hotel, but I didn't want to be anywhere near here. I just wanted to get out of town and to safety as quickly as possible. Mumbling and grumbling, Shadia agreed, and we left the bodies behind.

Barely a block away from the hotel, movement caught my eye. Two people were shambling their way toward us from the other end of the street. Even at this distance, I saw they were zombies by the way they walked. Slow and lumbering. They were both women, and both dressed in what looked like PJs. The one on the right was missing part of her cheek, the flesh within gray and decaying. The other had blood down the front of her shirt.

"We could turn around," I said. "Head up and over."

"No," Shadia answered. "We should continue toward the road."

"But what do we do with them?"

I felt it through the entire chair as Shadia changed her grip on the handle. "We try to go around," she said. "If not, we push them away."

I wasn't sure how we would get around them. We were on the sidewalk, which was thin and bumpy, and the road was clogged with cars. If I could walk, we could have weaved through them and to the other side, losing the zombies long before we met them, but that wasn't the case.

We met the women just past the halfway point of the street. Shadia had moved us to hug the walls of the buildings at our side, leaving a bit of room on the sidewalk. The zombies mirrored us, stumbling on the uneven bricks along the wall but never quite falling.

The woman with blood on her shirt moaned, her voice echoing inside my head and against the stone wall as she lunged forward, hands shooting out to grab at me.

Turning the ax, I pushed the blunt tip into her chest, pushing her back into the chest of the other woman. They both tumbled to the ground.

The chair jerked below me, and the armrest dug into my ribs as Shadia turned me to the side and pushed past the sprawling women. The one with the missing cheek reached out as we passed, her fingers getting caught in the wheel spokes and breaking off with a wet crunch.

"*Whalla,*" Shadia said in a low voice. I could hear the tears building in her throat.

I met the woman's eyes as we passed her and saw nothing in them but hunger. Even as her fingers broke off, there was no pain there. But if Shadia was going to cry, I couldn't cry. Then she would want to stop and comfort me, or she may think I was crying because I was too tired to move on and try to take me back to the hotel. I couldn't let that happen. We had to move forward. I wasn't sure if she heard it, but just at the edge of my hearing was the sound of moaning. Not that of the women we'd just left behind, but of a group of throats that must have noticed us despite being on another street. We had to get away from it.

So instead of crying, I looked down to make sure the fingers weren't still stuck in the wheel. They weren't; they'd fallen out, leaving hardly any evidence of what had happened. I sat back up again, trying to breathe calmly.

We reached the intersection the women had come from. The only way clear was to the left, but that would bring us back in a circle. Despite that, Shadia was turning me that way.

I grabbed the brakes and pushed them on. Behind me, Shadia almost tumbled over the chair.

"What are you doing?" she hissed. I could hear the tears behind the anger.

"We have to go over," I said, pointing at the clogged road. "We have to get down to the water, so we know where to find the road."

"But we can't."

I turned and met her eyes. They were wide, but not blank with tears or fear as I'd thought they might be. The set of her jaw told me she was holding it back. I reached up and cupped her cheek. "We have to," I repeated.

She looked into my eyes for a long moment before nodding. "OK, I'll carry you over first, then go back for the chair." I wanted to argue. I didn't want her to be on this side of the road alone, but I didn't see any other way to do it, so I nodded. "Give me the ax; you are not going to sit over there defenseless."

I only nodded again and handed her the weapon. She

wrapped the ax-head with her jacket before kneeling before me. I climbed onto her back, and she shot upright, moving forward almost before we were standing straight.

The cars were parked so tight she had to move sideways past the first pair to have a chance of getting through. As she turned, I looked back. The two zombie-women were back on their feet and making their way toward us again. They would be by the chair before Shadia got back to it. I wanted to urge her on but knew she couldn't move any faster, so I looked into the cars we passed. They were filled with stuff–animal cages and bags–but no people. A few doors were left open, telling of the panic that had made the drivers and passengers run away.

There were only two lanes, but it felt like we'd crossed a freeway by the time we were over. Shadia had to move down two cars while in the middle of the street to find a way through for us, and now the zombie women had reached the cars. They were leaning over the hood and roof of a car, clawing at the metal to get closer.

The moaning I'd heard earlier was louder as well, and I knew Shadia could hear it too. I saw it in the way her eyes jumped toward the noise every now and again. Instead of saying anything, she set me down on a power box against the wall and headed into the road again.

Clutching the ax to my chest, I could do nothing but watch as she weaved her way back to the other side. The women followed her step for step, staying across from her all the time.

Shadia stopped before the opening that would lead onto the sidewalk. She was turned away so I couldn't see her face, but I saw the set of her shoulders. They were determined but afraid. Her hands were knit against her thighs. After a long pause, she gripped the knife handle with one hand and supported herself against a car with the other. The women leaned over the hood in front of her, their fingers almost reaching her. If they took one more step to the side, they would find the opening and reach her, and Shadia would not be able to move fast enough to avoid them. I was about to tell her to just to come back, when she moved.

In one bound, she was on top of the car, stepping on the hand of the one with blood on her shirt. With the woman trapped, Shadia bent over and drove the knife into the woman's head.

My hands spasmed, and my ax fell from my slack grip and to the ground. Before the woman's body had fallen, Shadia moved on to the second zombie, making the same maneuver on her. As the dead body slipped out of sight, Shadia knelt on the hood of the car, her face turned away from me. Her shoulders and back were shaking like she was crying or throwing up. I wanted to go to her so bad I almost stumbled down from the power box. As if reading my thoughts, she turned her face toward me. Her eyes were dry and hard and met mine across the cars. I could see the threat in them. If I moved, she would be beyond angry. So I stayed put and watched as she climbed down from the car and grabbed the bags hanging on the chair.

She carried them over first, setting them by my feet. Then, without a word, she picked up my ax and handed it to me before going back for my chair. It took her longer to fold it up and maneuver it through the cars. In the end, she just pushed it on top of the hoods and roofs so it wouldn't get in her way.

While she worked, the moaning drew ever closer, and I saw movement in-between the cars the way we had come. Three people–zombies, I had to start thinking about them as zombies–had gathered on the opposite sidewalk to the one we had been on. They hadn't found a way through the cars yet and were trying to climb over the hoods without knowing they could climb. There was one making his way up the sidewalk on my side, black eyes glued on me, but he was far away.

Shadia finally got the chair to the asphalt and unfolded it. She didn't once look at me as she put the bags back in place and reached to help me into it. I grabbed her face and lifted it. Her eyes jumped to my throat.

"Shadia, look at me," I pleaded. I could hear the fear in my own voice and knew she could too. I saw guilt in her eyes at my words, but she couldn't look at me. "I'm so sorry," I said.

This made her look at me, a spark of anger in her set jaw now. "Why are you sorry?"

"'Cause you had to do that because of me. 'Cause I can't walk and take care of myself."

"That's nothing you should say sorry for. It's not your fault you're sick, so do not apologize for it, you hear me?" I nodded. She sighed and touched one of my hands. It was her left hand, not the one she had used to kill the zombies. "I would have had to do it sooner or later. Better now, so I know I can protect you." I wanted to tell her that she shouldn't have to protect me, that I should be able to do that myself, but she must have seen it in my eyes, for she shook her head. "You've already proven yourself. I needed to do that too. I needed to know if I could do it." She turned and looked at the man shambling his way toward us, then up at the group trying to find a way through the cars.

I wanted to argue that she shouldn't have to, that she was strong and kind, and killing zombies shouldn't be anything she should have to worry about. But I kept my mouth shut despite the tingling of adrenaline in my lips. Our world had changed. It was kill or be killed. The fact didn't make me any less sad for what Shadia had lost today.

When she looked back at me, I nodded, and she helped me into the chair.

Before either of the walking dead could reach us, we were on our way again.

Excerpt from Medical Notebook

No one knows where it started. The States blamed the Russians, and the Russians blamed the States. Great Britain and Asia blamed Europe, and Europe blamed Great Britan and Asia and Russia. In the end, it didn't matter where it started. It spread too fast.

At first, the people in charge thought it was a pandemic of a fast-moving flu virus. It seemed to spread the same way and started with typical flu symptoms–fever and a sore throat, dizziness, and headache. Then came nausea and vomiting. Then excreting blood. At this point, it was too late.

The doctors found worms in the tests they took, disproving the theory of a virus. The people infected were... infected with worms. When autopsied, the bodies were riddled with them.

The parasite killed its host within a few weeks. It made them come back from the dead within a few days.

6

I was starting to get a bad headache from the sharp sun, not to mention my whole body was sore from being carried over road after road. I really shouldn't complain, though. Shadia was the one lifting me up and setting me down. She was the one pushing me over uneven ground littered with people's discarded belongings. She ran back and forth through the maze of cars to get everything across. I hated myself for being tired and hurting, and at the same time, I couldn't help it. I would have loved for that to be our biggest problem. It wasn't.

We had to take a left turn at one point, then crossed three more streets, before we reached a point where we didn't dare cross anymore. The other side was teeming with the undead, groaning and moaning and clawing to reach us. Some of them were smaller than the others and found their way through the open car doors. They scraped their teeth against the glass, trying to get through. Some of the doors and windows were open, however, and the zombies crawled through and emerged closer to us.

If the zombies had just been in front, we could have crossed the road and continued along until we reached the freeway, but they weren't. We'd picked up a trail of them. They weren't smart enough to look for paths or fast enough to be any real threat, but we were now boxed in on three sides. Still not too close, not too dangerous, but enough that we were starting to panic.

"We can't keep going like this," I said and turned on the brakes of my chair. Shadia didn't fall over me this time, but I could hear her breathing quicken. She'd killed seven more zombies to keep me safe. I had only been allowed to take out one. "Sooner or later, they'll have us surrounded."

"They're not smart enough for that," she answered, her voice muffled because she was turned away.

"No, but they'll have more luck than us in this case."

"What do you want to do?"

"Either we continue as far as we can get before we look for a place to hide, or we find a place to hide and wait for them to disappear."

A silence fell between us, only broken by nails against metal and the sounds of the dead. It was starting to wear on my nerves, and I could feel frustrated tears coming on. Instead of letting them out, I found my pain pills and took one with a new Coca-Cola. After two big gulps, I handed it back to Shadia without looking. She took it, and I heard her drink deep. When I got it back, there were only a few sips left. I chugged them and threw the bottle in a nearby trashcan.

"You could have kept it," Shadia said. "Filled it with water or something."

"We have enough water."

It was true. We'd filled as many bottles of water as we could, only bringing the cola for me to drink as a boost when needed. The sugar and carbonate gave me a few extra seconds of a clear mind and feeling somewhat normal again.

"OK, we keep moving," I said, turning to look up at Shadia.

She met my eyes—as much as she could through my sunglasses. "But we don't go toward the water. We need to get out of town and find a road that's not clogged by cars."

"And how do we do that?"

"I honestly don't know, but we need to move, and soon." A zombie had just found its way past a car on the other side, leaving just one car between us. As if he led the way, the other zombies started following. Sooner or later, one of them would stumble on an easy path through.

"Right," Shadia said. "We move on and try to find a place in a few hours. You OK with that?"

I don't really have a choice. "Yeah. Let's go."

I opened the brakes, and Shadia pushed me forward. Instead of going over the cars and toward the group of dead people, she pushed on until we reached the farthest side of the sidewalk. There were zombies in-between the cars in front of us, but none close enough to stop us from crossing. The most important thing was that the other side of the void was clear.

We'd made crossing a kind of science by now, so I was over on the other side and leaning against the brick wall of a shop within a minute. Shadia hurried back and got our bags, then my chair. One of the zombies was one car closer to me now than before, but I was back in the chair and being pushed away long before it found the gap it needed to get to me. I couldn't help staring at it, though. It had been a young man at one point. Now he was grey and flabby, and his right hand was missing. It looked like someone had eaten it. The weirdest thing was the bright orange cross painted over his face, even covering his eyes, so when he looked at me, all I saw was orange. I wondered how he could see past that, or if they used their eyes at all.

Soon enough, we left him behind.

There were no zombies on the next street over or the next after that, but the moaning followed us.

"Where do you think they're all coming from?" I asked.

Shadia was quiet so long I wasn't sure she'd heard me, but finally, she spoke. "You noticed how most of them were young?" I nodded. "We're just a few blocks away from a high school." She didn't need to say anymore.

The schools, like the stadium, had been opened as refugee centers for those thrown out of their homes because their buildings were evacuated, or for the sick after the hospitals closed their doors, full past capacity. Some of the dead had been too small to be high school kids, but I guess they were younger siblings of the students. Families did whatever they could to stay together during something like this.

I wrapped my arms around my chest, trying to comfort myself. The thought of family gnawed at the wall I'd formed around the memory and grief of my own family. I hadn't been a big part of it for years because of my health, but I still loved them.

The street we were currently on was one of the main roads through town, so we could walk a long way without having to cross another road. That was good. I could sense that Shadia needed some time to herself. We may be less than a meter apart, but with me in the chair and her behind, we might as well be in two separate worlds.

I never wanted kids, but Shadia did. We'd talked about adopting before I got sick, but her dreams were flushed down the toilet because of my poor health. Her head must be full of thoughts and memories of seeing those dead children. What was she thinking? Was she happy we never grew too close to a little soul just to lose it to this world? Or was she sorry we never got the chance, and would rather have loved and lost, than not loved at all? I knew, somewhere in her heart, she always hoped I would wake up healthy and fine one day, and we could resume our lives where the cancer had paused them; that we could start looking into adopting again. Now, that dream would never happen.

Even when we reached another road that needed crossing, we didn't say a word. I felt her heartbeat through her back and against my chest as she carried me, but we might not even have been touching.

We reached another road. Just up to our right was a roundabout. There were no zombies there that I could see, hear, or smell. To our left, another road went toward the water. If we followed it, we would get to one of the most open roads in the city, and it should lead us right to the freeway.

I turned and looked up at Shadia. She met my eyes. Hers were a little distant like she was lost in thought, but she blinked and came back. "I was thinking," she said. "There is a bike road along the freeway. That should be free of cars, right?"

"What if there are zombies?"

"There might be zombies on every other road. We don't know."

"You think we'll make it there?"

"Yes."

"OK, then we do that."

Her grim face was frozen for a second before she smiled. It lit up her eyes and made her look alive.

7

We followed the sidewalk around the corner of the building and down to another street, which we crossed without issue. The road continued unobscured for a while before we reached another road to cross. Here, the cars weren't as packed, and Shadia could maneuver me while in the chair to get through. It made the whole process a lot easier. My hands had acquired a weak shaking, but it didn't seem to get worse as we moved along, so I tried to relax.

I'd gotten so used to the groaning and moaning of the zombies that I didn't notice right away when it got louder. I don't think Shadia did either. We did notice when the wind turned and brought the scent with it.

As the smell hit, Shadia slowed our process to a crawl and grunted in disgust. The smell seemed to fill my mouth and nose, and for a moment, I was completely lost in it.

"What street are we on?" Shadia asked, bringing me back to reality.

From somewhere ahead, a heavy, rhythmic thumping sounded again and again and again.

I shook my head, trying to dislodge the smell. "Løvenskiold," I said, looking at the street name on one of the buildings.

Shadia stopped. "Sha?"

Turning to look, I saw her eyes were jumping around the street in front of us, and she was chewing on her bottom lip.

"It should be OK," she said, more to herself than to me. "If we haven't seen them yet, they should be confined."

"Sha? What's going on?"

She snapped out of her thoughts but didn't take her eyes off the street. Instead, she started walking briskly. "Eyes forward. Be prepared for anything."

I turned but said her name again, worry and fear creeping into my voice. She didn't answer but pushed a little faster.

The thumping grew louder.

Just ahead, someone had put up a temporary chain link fence, and an arm shot through the links, small fingers clawing at the air. Without slowing, Shadia pushed me as far away from the wall as she could, so close to the cars a mirror smacked into my arm and almost threw the chair off balance.

We reached the chain link fence, and I saw children, teens, and adults, pushed up against it. They were all undead. One girl was dressed in a My Little Pony sleeping gown. A boy was in a Spider-Man set. A woman was in her bathrobe, and a man was naked but for a set of slacks. They all were either in their socks or had naked feet. Their fingers grasping through the fence to get at us. A few more of the smaller zombies got their arms through the links and reached.

"Shadia," I said, barely above a whisper.

"Eyes ahead, *habibi*," she said, her voice strained.

I tore my gaze away from the undead, but not before I glimpsed something through their ranks: a bloody mess on the ground behind them. I wasn't sure, but it looked like a zombie with its stomach torn open. It even lacked its legs and most of its arms, but its head was still there, and it was tossing back and forth, clacking its teeth and looking at us with empty black eyes.

Bile rose in my throat. I couldn't stop it this time and threw up over the side of the chair. Fingers brushed the top of my head, and I jerked back, barely remembering to hold onto my hat and hitting my chin on the armrest and biting my tongue. Shadia never slowed down.

I retched, but nothing more came up. Shadia mumbled in Arabic and stopped so fast I almost flew out of the chair.

"Kit, come on, I need you with me."

The urgency in her voice made me look up, blinking away tears. The road in front of us was blocked by a trailer. It had slid out of control and spun, so the back of it was embedded in the building on the other side of the road. Its nose was centimeters away from the building on the other side, the opening too small for anyone to get through. The way forward was blocked.

I turned, looking down the sidewalk. We could probably push down that way, but if I remembered the streets correctly, it would take us away from the road we needed to reach the freeway. It was clear.

The chain link fence wobbled as zombies pushed against it, and the thumping sounded faster and clearer, but I couldn't place it.

Behind me, Shadia was murmuring to herself. Before I could ask what she was saying, she spoke up. "We need to climb."

"What?" I turned to stare at her, but she wasn't looking at me. Her eyes were on the trailer.

"We need to climb the trailer and get to the other side." I wanted to argue that there was no way I could get up on that thing, but I knew there really wasn't anything to argue about. Either we climbed, or we risked being taken by the zombies behind us, or new ones somewhere down the road.

"OK," I said.

Shadia squeezed my shoulder and pushed me into the road, toward the nose of the trailer. Cars had stopped a little away, trying not to crash into it, making it easier for us to move.

The thumping grew louder, and I realized it was coming from somewhere on the other side of the trailer. I was about to stop the chair, but Shadia's words ran through my mind. It was this or risk meeting zombies somewhere else. I didn't stop the chair, but let myself roll onward.

The stench was so strong I thought I might throw up again, but there was nothing left in my stomach. I was just glad the pain meds had kicked in before I spit them back up again.

"You first," Shadia said as we reached the trailer.

Stone scraped against stone behind us, and we both turned. The zombies were pushed up against the fence, moving it forward with their weight. It would either topple or break enough so they could spill through an opening. No time to argue. No time to doubt. Just move.

I pushed out of the chair and almost fell on top of the trailer. Before I had time to right myself, Shadia wrapped her arms around my waist and lifted me up. I grabbed at the line between the window and the hood and somehow got support for my feet from the front lights. Appendages shaking from the effort, and with Shadia helping as much as she could, I managed to get onto the front window. I was on my own from there.

As I tried to climb, the muscles in my chest constricted and starting to cramp. On the ground, Shadia found a rope in one of our bags and folded up the chair. She tied the rope around the bags and chair alike before tying the other end of the rope around her waist.

The sound of metal scraping against metal grated against my ears, followed by the sound of stone against stone, as part of the fence was pushed far enough out to lose contact with the rest. Zombies spilled through it, seeming surprised to be free before they started moving toward Shadia. She didn't hesitate but climbed after me. Long before the zombies reached us, she was up on the roof of the cockpit.

"Come on, Kit."

I was panting, using every ounce of willpower and strength I had not to fall down. I knew the zombies could reach me. They would be able to grab my legs and pull me down to them, but I couldn't move. Or, that wasn't right. My entire body was shaking so much it almost dislodged me from my perch. I was afraid the shaking would take control if I moved.

"You have to move, Kit. Take my hand."

I managed to turn my head to look at Shadia. She was reaching down for me, her hand resting on top of mine, ready to grab me if I loosened my grip. Gritting my teeth, I forced my hand to turn. It jerked and danced, trying to get away from Shadia's hand, but she grabbed me around the wrist and pulled.

"Kick for me," she said, and I did. With that boost, she was able to pull me onto the cockpit.

I slumped against her, my legs and arms dancing uncontrolled around me as I concentrated on breathing. My chest was vibrating, my diaphragm so tight there was hardly any room in my lungs for air.

"OK, it's OK," Shadia whispered against my hair, hugging

me with both arms and legs.

On the ground, the zombies reached the chair and walked right past it, starting to claw at the car. The thumping was so close now, it felt like it was making the car vibrate every time it sounded, but that might just have been me.

After almost half an hour, my shaking calmed down enough that Shadia dared loosen her grip a little. All the while, she had been murmuring to me, trying to calm me. We both knew the shakes had to run their course, but we also knew that if I stressed or grew afraid it would get worse.

"Will you fall off if I put you down for a second?" Shadia asked, her lips brushing against my forehead.

"Why?" I managed through chattering teeth.

"I want to get our bags so I can find your eye-mask and headphones. Give you some rest."

I couldn't help the hoarse laugh. "Rest? Up here?" She didn't answer, but I knew she was serious. "Why?"

"Because I don't think we're getting anywhere else any time soon."

"Why?"

Her eyes jumped past me. I would have expected her to look at the group of zombies that had formed at the nose of the trailer, clawing and trying to get to us, but she was looking behind me.

I turned in her arms, my head jerking back and forth three times before I was able to hold it still and look. The road was a mess of cars that had crashed into each other, into the side of the trailer, and into the buildings on either side of the street. I finally saw where the thumping was coming from. A zombie lay squeezed between two cars, it's bottom half was caught by the warped metal, and it was hitting the car in front of it, trying to claw its way free. I could see it had already started to tear from rot; its upper body would soon leave the legs behind. And it wasn't the only one. Three more zombies were stuck in the cars, trying to break free. But there were even more of them wandering freely. They filled the street, and I saw bones on the ground, not a morsel of flesh or blood left on them, picked clean by the zombies now trying to climb the cars to get to us.

I turned back and looked at the zombies that had gotten through the fence.

"Oh," I said as Shadia pulled me so close I had trouble breathing again.

We were surrounded.

8

As my muscles calmed down, I slid out of Shadia's arms and wrapped into as small a ball as possible. Shadia rested her hand on my shoulder, her fingers like ice against my flushed skin, until she was sure I wouldn't slide off the car and into the arms of the waiting zombies, before she stood.

I wanted to look at her, to see how she was doing, but kept my eyes closed. I heard her walk to the edge of the roof, making the metal under us vibrate. Her breathing strained, and something soft hit the side of the car enough to send a jolt through my bones. Shadia mumbled in Arabic before she started moving again. She walked to the side; then, she was gone. I almost opened my eyes, but I could still hear her breathing and her steps, so I didn't. I trusted her.

After a lot of sounds and cursing, in Norwegian, English, and Arabic, she came onto the roof of the car again. By the force of her first step, I thought she might have jumped from the trailer.

"Here," she said as she sat beside me again, her shadow falling over my face.

"Thanks."

I blindly reached out, but her hands closed around mine

and lay them down against the warm car before her fingers carefully touched my temples. I squeezed my eyes shut as she pulled off the hat and my glasses, shortly followed by her lifting my head just enough to slide the sleeping mask over my eyes. It was soft and smelled faintly of lavender. The scent immediately made me more tired, and I couldn't help suspecting that Shadia had brought a bag of lavender to help me sleep. Next, she put something soft under my head as a pillow. It smelled like her, and I thought it was her jacket.

"I can't put in the earbuds for you," she said.

I snorted a laugh, remembering the time she tried it and almost pierced my eardrum as my head jerked at the sudden feeling.

"It's OK," I said. "I'd rather listen to you anyway."

"Listen to me?"

"I can hear your breathing, almost hear your heart. That's better than the static of headphones."

She didn't answer but took my twitching hand in hers again.

We stayed there for a long while, her waiting and me slipping in and out of a kind of hazy darkness. We called it The Fog. It happened when I was too tired for my body to be able to push itself any longer, and it just shut down. It was a long time since it had happened at the same time as a seizure. It scared me just as much now as it had the first time, but I had to push that fear deep down and not let it take root. If I did, the seizure would get worse. The seizure was a physical reaction to my body being pushed too far, but it could be affected by my mental state.

Every time I woke from The Fog, the first thing I heard was the moaning and groaning and clawing of the undead. Some part of me would start dancing a little harder as my breathing shortened from fear. Then Shadia would squeezer my hand and start talking about something. It could be the weather or what she wanted to do when we got to the cabin or even gossip about an author she liked. It calmed me.

Through it all, my muscles felt like they would burst with lactic acid, and my bones felt like something was gnawing on them, like someone kept poking my skin with warm needles. It was nothing new, but it hurt as if fresh every time, and I had to hold back so I wouldn't cry from the pain. If I cried, Shadia would be more afraid, and that would only make this harder.

After slipping in and out of The Fog seven times, I woke to a still body. I could feel the shakes in my muscles and waited for the slightest hint that they'd start again, but I stayed still. No one was gnawing on my bones, and no one was poking me with needles. I was left with a tingling sensation running up and down my skin, and muscles that felt empty and airy, except for the hint of a seizure lying deep within, waiting.

"How are you feeling?" Shadia asked, her hand squeezing mine again. She had never let go, even when my hand spasmed and the grip grew so tight it must have hurt.

"Hollow," I answered, my voice almost as empty as my body. I was so tired.

Somewhere in the back of my mind, I knew we had to do something about our situation. We couldn't stay out here during the night, and I could feel the early evening chill set in, even if the car was still warm from the sun. Despite all that, I couldn't bring myself to care. I was too tired, and I just wanted to sleep.

"I know, *habibi*," Shadia said, stroking my hair with her free hand. She didn't say that we had to move; she didn't tell me the obvious. She was willing to risk staying out here to stay with me.

I turned my face toward her and considered pulling on the sunglasses, but instead used my free hand to lift the lower side of the mask so I could look at her with one eye. Her brow was wrinkled and her jaw set, but she smiled with her lips if not her eyes as we looked at each other.

"You should–" I began, but was cut off by a yell.

"Hello there!"

Shadia stiffened and turned so fast she almost pulled my arm with her. The sudden sound sent a shiver through my body, a forewarning of another seizure, but I managed to stop it before it got a firm grip. I felt it just under my skin, but as long as I kept my mind on not shaking, I could hold it. I hoped.

"Who's there?" Shadia called.

"Just me." It was a male voice. Youngish. "You need any help?"

Shadia looked down at me, and I met her eye before she let my hand go and stood. "Yes."

"OK, just hang on." Some kind of scuffling sounded before the man spoke again. "What's up with her?"

"She's had a seizure and is sick. Will you still help?"

"Why wouldn't I? Here, climb up."

"She can't climb."

A silence before: "Then we'll pull her up."

"She can't hold on."

"Then tie her in before you climb up, and we'll pull after that."

He didn't sound angry or anything; more like he was unsure if this was a smart idea. If it was because of me and my condition, or something else, I didn't know. Shadia told him to hold on before she crouched in front of me again. She didn't say anything but held out my sunglasses. I let her pull off the eye-mask and push on my glasses and hat before she helped me to my feet. A small vibration started in my legs and arms, and I had no chance of controlling it this time.

"It's OK. We've got this," Shadia whispered in my ear before she pulled me into her arms like a prince carrying a princess and started walking. I clung to her as my left leg started to kick the air.

She continued whispering to me as she walked to the edge of the car and jumped. It wasn't far to the trailer roof, but it must have been hard for her to jump with me in her arms like that, not to mention landing without toppling with my added weight, huffing and puffing with concentration, but she did it. She walked to the end of the trailer, and I looked up despite the sun.

A rope with knots every meter or so hung over the edge of the roof, and I saw the shadow of someone looking down at us. Probably our savior.

Shadia lowered me to the trailer and set me up straight. My foot was dancing again, but not as bad as earlier, and she hardly glanced at it as she took the end of the rope and tied it around my waist.

"When we pull, you have to hold on, OK? Or you'll slip out." Her voice was stern but low. It was the voice she used when she was afraid for me but worked hard not to let me know. I nodded. She kissed my forehead before she stood, and I had to close my eyes against the glare of the sun.

Curling into a small ball, I listened to her move about a little before she came to my side again.

"I'm climbing up now," she called to the man on the roof,

and to let me know I would be alone a little while.

My hand jerked, wanting to reach for Shadia. Then the rope started moving against my cheek. I listened to Shadia breathe and move above me before the man said something I couldn't hear. Shadia answered in just as low a voice.

"We're lifting our stuff now, Kit. Ok?" I gave a shaky thumbs up. More sounds followed, and I recognized the sound of the wheelchair scraping against stone. More muffled words, then: "OK, *habibi*, hold on!"

Unfurling, I gripped the rope as best I could, just over a knot so I wouldn't slip. My fingers were stiff and the muscles in my wrists didn't want to work with me, but I managed somehow. I yelled that I was ready. Within seconds, the rope grew taut in my hands, and I was lifted from the trailer, knots digging into my sides, almost numbing my legs.

"You have to look," Shadia called, "so you don't hit the wall."

Tears spilled as I opened one eye and fought to keep it open despite the bright sun. It was a good thing, for I almost hit the brick wall, but one hand shot out and pushed me away. Above, Shadia called encouraging words, but her voice was strained.

I reached the edge of the roof without any more problems and scrambled to grab it. A pale hand with long fingers and orange paint spots grabbed mine. I stared at that hand for a heartbeat before it pulled me up, and I all but fell over the edge.

The hand was gone, but Shadia was there, untying the rope. She kept asking how I was doing and if I hurt, and I answered in a kind of daze. I could feel The Fog coming again and tried to fight it, but my sight was growing dimmer by the second.

Shadia pulled me to my feet, and with the help of our savior, I was moved into my chair. I could feel the stranger's clammy skin against my fingers and desperately wanted to clean them, but I couldn't speak, much less do the cleaning, so I curled into a small, jerking ball instead. The Fog slipped in around me.

9

My memory after that is a mess of lights, smells, feelings, and The Fog.

I remember sitting in my chair, curled into a ball, and shaking as the wheels rattled over uneven ground and the sun bit at my neck. Shadia was talking, but her words swam in and out of focus. Sometimes, a male voice would answer, but I didn't always remember why there was a man with us.

Then the biting sunlight was gone, and I lay wrapped around Shadia. She carried me like a child. My face pressed against her shoulder, and my feet kept hitting something whenever they kicked out.

"Almost there," the male voice said. I could hear worry dripping from every letter, and wondered what he was worried about.

Shadia answered something I didn't catch. The rumble of her voice ran through my body as a shake of its own, and I was lost to The Fog again.

When I came to next, I lay on something hard. It smelled of mildew and wet stone, and the air was thick and clammy. But most importantly: my muscles were calm and still. I could feel my arms and legs splayed around me like dead weight. I wasn't sure I could move them even if I wanted to, and I didn't want to.

Instead, I stayed completely still, just breathing and listening to the low voices. Shadia and the man who had helped us. They were talking about an experiment of some sort. I didn't understand half of it, but it scared me.

My breathing must have changed with my fear, for the conversation stopped. Shadia was by my side in a heartbeat.

"Kit?" she whispered, her voice soft as puppy fur against my cheek. Her fingers were like pure rain against my forehead as she brushed my hair out of my eyes. I opened them and looked at her. She smiled, but it didn't quite reach her eyes. "Do you need anything?"

I parted my lips to answer with a joke but was too tired. Instead, I croaked something that sounded like 'ouch'. Shadia's smile grew a little more real.

"Hold on."

She disappeared from sight for a few seconds before she maneuvered herself to sit behind me, my head in her lap, and held a bottle to the corner of my mouth. I opened my lips and let her dribble some water onto my tongue. Swallowing hurt, but the cooling that followed was so worth it. When I opened my eyes again, Shadia held a small pill in front of my face. One of my pain pills. I wanted to ask if it had been three hours since I took the last one, but I trusted Shadia would know. I opened my mouth again and let her place the pill on my tongue before she dribbled more water into my mouth.

My eyes closed on their own, and I stayed with my head in Shadia's lap until I fell asleep.

I woke again at nine p.m. when the alarm on my wristwatch beeped. Shadia helped me take the medication I needed before

I fell back into The Fog.

Days passed this way. I woke to my alarm at nine a.m. and p.m., and Shadia helped me take my meds. Even on the second day, when I could do it myself, she insisted on helping. So I wouldn't strain myself.

I didn't soil myself. When I woke and needed to go, Shadia carried me to a hole cut in the floor leading into the sewers. It smelled like death and everything rotten that ever lived. Whoever made the hole had also added a chair without a seat, and Shadia helped me pull down my jeans before she left me to do my stuff. She still had to help me up when I was done, but I got to keep the idea of dignity, at least. These trips were usually so exhausting I fell asleep the moment Shadia laid me down again.

Almost every time I woke, she was sitting by my side, reading on her Kindle, but the moment I stirred or my breathing changed, she'd put it away to help me.

On the third day, after a bathroom trip, I wasn't so tired anymore. Instead of falling asleep, I looked around as Shadia curled up beside me, keeping me company on the small mat we'd been sleeping on.

We were in a small room with concrete walls, floor, and ceiling. When we went to the bathroom, we passed through two bigger rooms before arriving at the hole in the floor. All the walls were naked and dripping with condensation, and there were big metal doors between each of the rooms, but only one of them was closed. It was in the last room before the toilet, and it looked like a vault door one might see in a movie. Cheap lamps lined the ceiling, most of them blinking unevenly. They were fueled by a generator chugging away in a corner. My guess was that we were in a basement or a bomb-shelter.

The town was full of them, after all. My chair stood by the door, strangely clean compared to its surroundings. Our bags were in the small room with us.

Never once had I seen any sign of our savior. I knew Shadia talked to him every morning and evening, but he disappeared before I went to the bathroom.

It was now close to the evening of our fourth day. If not for my medication routines, I would have no idea how long we'd been down there.

"Who is he?" I asked, staring at the wall and playing with Shadia's fingers. My body didn't feel like a seizure was waiting to happen anymore, and most of my pains were dull and almost non-existent.

"Who?" Shadia asked, voice sleepy.

"The guy who helped us. Why don't I ever see him?"

She sighed and curled her fingers in mine, stopping my playing with them. "Because I was afraid meeting him would be too much in the state you were in. You know how you can get with new people."

It was true. After I got sick, meeting people became a chore. I put on a mask and smiled and faked it until I fell apart, crying from exhaustion and pain.

"Fine," I answered. "But what about now? I've rested, and I'm starting to get bored."

Shadia smiled against my neck. "Fine. I'll introduce you tonight if you're still awake."

"Why tonight? Where does he go?"

"To do his experiments."

"What kind?"

"He can tell you himself. Now try to get some sleep."

"No, then I won't meet him."

"He won't be back for hours yet. Sleep."

She kissed my neck, and I shivered, wanting to do everything else with her other than rest, but I closed my eyes anyway.

"See? I told you fresh air would help," Shadia said as she hurried up the steps before me.

I wobbled after her, taking one slow step at a time.

When we got into the building, I was taking the elevator. She might think I had to use my legs so they wouldn't wither away, but she had no idea how much it hurt just moving them.

Shadia waited on the top step and reached out a hand to help me up the last one. She didn't let my hand go as she unlocked the door.

"Mother used to say that good energy breed more good energy, and I think that might be the case here. You have to admit you feel better now than you did before we left?" That I couldn't argue with, but she didn't give me a chance to answer, so it didn't matter. "I think you look better, at least. You've got some color in your cheeks again. I think you might even have a tan."

Her eyes kept jumping between me and the elevator as we walked, and I realized that she was talking so much because she was worried.

"I'm fine," I panted, gripping my cane to not topple over at each step. The cane had helped a lot around the apartment, but it didn't seem to have done anything today. My legs felt like heavy bags of laundry. For every step, a spark of pain ran through my muscles, and they felt ... slow. Like they were a lagging video game.

Shadia had dragged me to the park, and while I mostly sat on the grass and petted the dogs that came over, the walk and tram-rides back and forth had drained me. It didn't help that my mind was one big, foggy landscape from the sun, smells, and sounds.

The elevator dinged, and I felt the sound vibrate in my bones. Shadia stepped inside, helping me as she went. As soon as the doors closed, I leaned against her and let her carry my weight a little. The sudden release on my legs hurt almost as much as if I'd stayed on them but in a different way.

I'd tried to describe the subtle differences in pain to my doctor once. He just stared at me with worried eyes and said plainly that he didn't understand. How could he? How could anyone, unless they lived with it?

The elevator stopped and the doors opened with a hiss. I pushed away from Shadia, and she stepped out of the elevator, still holding my hand. I tried to move after her, but my legs wouldn't listen.

"Kit?" Shadia stopped and turned, her eyes narrow. I tried moving my legs again, but nothing happened. "Are you coming?"

My hand had turned white in hers and around the cane's head as I gripped them both with all the strength I had. I tried channeling that strength into my legs, tried with every fiber of my being to move them, but nothing happened. They started shaking, but I wasn't sure if it was in response to my commands or from standing too long. Dizziness was creeping through the back of my mind, but my fear kept it at bay.

"I can't," I said, voice barely louder than a breath as I looked up and met Shadia's gaze. "I can't move my legs."

10

When I opened my eyes again, it was to the beeping of my alarm. I could still smell my own fear, but instead of dwelling on it, I looked around.

Shadia was there, as always, pills in one hand and a bottle of water in the other. I took my medication dutifully, but couldn't help looking at her expectantly. Her eyes were shining. As soon as my meds were out of her hands, she started bustling about our stuff, her lips twisting every now and again.

No way was I going to ask. She had said I could meet our host if I was awake when he returned, and I was awake now. I was not going to ask her if he was back and I could meet him. Nope. No way was she going to win this game. I would just lie here and maybe close my eyes a little and wait for her to … no. If I closed my eyes, I might fall asleep again.

I let out a groan. "Fine! Is he here? Can I meet him now?"

Shadia's twisting lips grew into a grin, and she gave a small noise of triumph. "Yes, he's here. André, you can come in now."

Someone moved in the doorway, and I pushed up onto my elbows. Shadia rushed to let me rest against her, and I let her fuss over me as I took in the man standing before us. He couldn't be much older than us, and he was way thinner than me but as tall as Shadia. It made him look like a stick. He was as pale as me, with strawberry blond hair that reached just past his hips. It hung in a loose ponytail, and I couldn't help but admire it. His eyes were small and blue, and they kept jumping to mine before they jumped to a spot between his feet. He wore a threadbare t-shirt with some anime girl on it, worn jeans, and even more tired sneakers. The only thing that looked new on him was the scarf wrapped around his neck.

He drew a deep breath and finally met my eyes properly, holding them. "Hi," he said, stepping forward with his right hand out. "My name is André. You must be Kit."

Shadia helped me up to a sitting position. "Yeah, I am. Hey, André."

His grip was surprisingly strong, considering how small his hand was. It was dry, but I still pushed my palm against the blanket when we let go, trying to remove the feeling of his skin. He rocked back and forth on his toes a few times before he sighed and rushed out of the room.

I turned to look at Shadia, but she only shook her head. Before I had turned around again, André was back, a dried bierwurst in hand. The scent of garlic reached us before he did, and I almost gagged.

"So," André said, peeling the plastic from around the dried sausage with great concentration and plumping down on the floor by my feet. "She tells me you two are like a thing?" I raised an eyebrow that he didn't see because he was so focused on the food in his hand. When I didn't answer right away, he nodded and continued, "that's nice. Nice. I'm not a thing. With anyone, I mean. Anyway. So what's your problem?" He finally met my eyes and he pointed at me with the bierwurst.

My eyebrows rose. "My problem?"

60

He jerked his hands and head in an imitation of a seizure before he pointed over his shoulder with the sausage. Probably at my chair. "Why you in a chair and why you are twisting and such? She won't tell me. Just said you were sick."

I guessed 'she' meant Shadia. This guy was really hard to talk to, never keeping his eyes on one spot and talking low but fast, like he was afraid we would hear him.

Shadia snaked her hand around me and took one of mine. I'd been pulling at my fingers, but she stopped me by showing she was there for me. "I've got Myalgic Encephalomyelitis," I said, almost stumbling over the words.

"What's that?"

"A neurological condition."

"Sounds weird. Why do you have that?"

I bit down on the laughter welling in my throat. I couldn't keep back the smile. André blinked a few times before he started eating his bierwurst, not looking at me anymore.

"I have it as a long-term side effect of chemotherapy. I survived Lymphoma some years ago but continued getting sicker and sicker after the treatment was completed. In the end, the doctors gave me the diagnosis for M.E.. What a price to pay for survival, eh?" I motioned to my legs as spite snuck its way into my voice.

Shadia squeezed my hand and tried to draw me against her, as if she could protect me with her body. André had almost finished his sausage, not seeming able to stop once he started, but he stopped now and stared openly at me. It was the longest his eyes had rested on me so far.

"Anyway," I said, trying to break the heavy silence that hung between us. "Shadia said you were doing some kind of experiments?"

This seemed to shake him out of his stupor and he hurriedly finished eating the bierwurst before he began speaking. "'Experimenting' may be a bit too heavy a term. Observations would be more like it, you know."

"OK. Observing what?"

"The walking dead, of course."

Excerpt from Medical Notebook

No one knows who patient zero was, or even where they came from. What we do know is that the sickness sprang up in major cities across the world within one weekend.

At first, no one knew it was any different than the flu, but it spread fast. Within weeks, most of the countries in Europa had shut down, trying to contain it. America was in upheaval, every State running according to their own rules but none able to contain it. China cut off from the rest of the world first, shortly followed by Japan.

Everyone tried to figure out where it started, but everyone had different suggestions. The best minds in the world raced to find a cure. They were too slow.

11

His words seemed to hang between us like a bad smell. Looking at Shadia, I could tell she already knew what André was about to tell me, but I couldn't tell if she approved or not.

"OK," I said again.

André seemed to take this as confirmation and swung the rucksack he was wearing around his shoulder. As he talked, he looked through it. "The reason I was at the street where I found you is because it's one of my observation points. While some of the walkers come and go as they please, those stuck between the cars don't go anywhere, and that makes it a lot easier to observe how they function. Before you two came along, I used the ones at the school as well, but they're all gone now."

"Sorry," I mumbled.

He pulled a notebook from the rucksack. "No matter." He pushed the book toward me. "They would have found something to chase sooner or later, I guess. Or they might have stayed and rotted. Who knows?"

I don't know what I'd expected the notebook to be about, but I was totally unprepared for the pictures and notes that met me. The first few pages weren't so bad. André had filled them with everything we knew about the undead from the news. It wasn't much, but André must have been a fan of zombie shows, for he had written possible similarities to some of them, and tried to use that as a way to learn as much about the zombies as he could. Some of his conclusions had to be wrong, but others seemed plausible, like the parasite eggs spreading through water.

"But why didn't anyone see the eggs? They can't be that small." Shadia pointed out.

André shrugged. "How do parasite eggs get through anywhere? They've been getting into us humans for thousands of years, you know."

"OK," Shadia pulled out the word. "Then how did it get in the water in the firstplace? And all around the world almost at the same time?"

"My theory is that the eggs wouldn't hatch before ideal conditions, which might be based on temperature or weather or who knows what! So the eggs might have been spreading for years, and then something in the atmosphere triggered them to wake up."

"Or they may have been spread by humans," Shadia said.

André nodded. "We just don't have enough info."

"If this is right," I said, tapping the page with my finger, "how come you're not sick?"

Shadia snickered, and André blushed before he stuck a hand into his rucksack and pulled out a Monster can. "I only drink energy drinks," he said, not meeting my eyes, before pushing the can back into his pack. "She told me you two only drink water from a cooler?"

I glanced at Shadia before I nodded. "Or, mostly? I only drink from a cooler, but Sha sometimes drinks coffee and tea at work, don't you?"

She nodded, but before she could answer, André scooted forward, his eyes big and intense. "She told me, and I think that answers a few other questions."

"Which ones?"

"That the eggs die when boiled." He snatched the book from my hands and leafed through it. "I haven't really met anyone else who survived, but I know there are people in the city."

"If you haven't met them, how do you know they're there?" I asked.

He snorted. "They aren't hard to find. They've set up in Vigeland Parken."

Shadia's hand found its way to my shoulder, and I felt the small tremor in it. "How many?"

"Around fifty or so? Ah, here! This is what I was looking for." He turned the book back to face me. On the page was a polaroid picture of a group of skinny but clearly alive people walking around between the statues of Vigeland Park. "They are all alive. I couldn't believe they all avoided drinking tap water for some reason or another. It's too big a coincidence that they also know each other, don't you think?" Before we could answer, he continued. "So I kept an eye on them, you know, and this has led to another conclusion. The parasite needs fresh meat to survive. Without meat, it just shrivels away."

"And how did this group of people lead you to that conclusion?" Shadia asked. She had scooted to sit behind me now, letting me rest against her. "If you haven't talked to them, I mean."

He fidgeted again. "Well, I kind of listened in, you know? The thing is, they're like a cult. According to what I could hear, they used to be the members of this super-healthy yoga studio uptown. If you didn't follow the studio's rules, you were kicked out."

"And how do you know that?" I asked.

Still not meeting our eyes, he started tugging at his long hair. "Well, you see … when it all started out, I met one of them, you know?"

"One of who?"

"One of those people from the cult. I was out to look at the Zs, you know, when I saw him. He was in trouble like you two were, and I helped him. After, he told me to stay away from the park and the people there."

"Why?"

"Well, according to him, you know, they didn't accept new members unless they reformed to their rules. Or the rules of the leader of the studio. He wasn't really a part of the studio but followed part of their rules to support his wife. The leader collected everyone when the city evacuation started. He claimed they had been chosen by some God or other, and that's why they didn't get sick. Anyway, he wanted every marriage to be dissolved and the group to repopulate the earth. This guy I met, Harold, and his wife didn't want to go along with it, so they were kicked out."

"But how did that lead you to conclude that the parasite needs fresh meat to survive?" Shadia asked. Something in what André had said tickled at the back of my brain, but I couldn't put my finger on what it was.

"One of their rules is to be vegetarian. They don't eat meat, and so they don't provide food for the parasite. Think about it. What other animals were affected?"

"I don't know. I can't really remember anything from the

news about that."

"Cats and dogs. Rats and foxes. Animals that eat meat, you know? They had this whole thing at the beginning where they thought the sickness spread from meat, right? But they didn't find any parasites or anything in the stomachs of cows or chickens, but they did find it in the stomachs of pigs on a few farms. On farms where they fed them with some kind of meat. The eggs are everywhere, but without fresh meat, they don't mature, and so the worm is never born."

Shadia had wrapped her arms around me and was squeezing a little too tight. She was afraid, and no wonder. What André was talking about was scary. "Do they all come back? Those animals? Like we do?"

André shook his head. "I don't think so. I haven't seen any zombie dogs or cats, at least, although I think I might have seen a rat."

"Why not?"

"Maybe they're not big enough to support the parasite? Or they're somehow harder to control? I don't know yet, although I would love to catch a few animals and test them."

"What? You want to make animals that may have escaped the parasite sick?"

He shrugged. "That's how science is made."

Finally, what had been itching at my brain clicked. "Wait," I said, stopping Shadia in the middle of an argument for why André should find some other way. I couldn't say I disagreed with her, but I needed to know. "What happened to his wife?"

"Whose wife?" André asked, but he didn't meet my eyes.

Shadia stiffened even more behind me.

"That guy, Harold. The former members of the cult. You said his wife got kicked out with him? Where was she when you saved him?"

André busied himself looking through his pack. When he came up again, he'd brought another sausage with him. I wanted to hit it out of his hand, but he didn't do anything with it. Just looked at it as he answered. "She was taken by the Zs two days before, he told me. He was out there, wanting them to eat him as well, but for some reason, he couldn't find any when he needed them. Then I came along, and he doubted himself."

"What happened to him?" Shadia asked, voice barely higher than a whisper.

André shrugged. "I don't know. I brought him back here to rest as I did with you, but when I got back after my trip out the following day, he was gone. I haven't seen him since."

The silence between us was no longer as hard as it had been before the conversation started, but it was still heavy. Finally, André sighed and started removing the plastic around the sausage. This one smelled of chili rather than garlic.

"So you think we escaped the parasite because we didn't drink water from the tap unless it was boiled, and you didn't drink water at all, and the people at Vigeland because they didn't eat meat?" I asked. André nodded, his eyes flicking up and meeting mine for a few seconds. "What else did you figure out?"

He took a bite of the Bierwurst and chewed it to pieces before he found another notebook. "I keep an eye on the Zs to see how they evolve."

"Evolve?" I asked.

Taking the book before I could open it, Shadia leaned forward and put a hand on the cover. "I've looked inside this one, and it can be rough, OK Kit?" she whispered.

"What kind of rough?" I asked.

"Close-ups of ... things."

"Those are in the back," André said, but he wasn't looking at us again. This would get old fast. "I'm using the front to observe the actual walking dead, or the stuck but still alive dead, you know? If you want to see some of the stuff they leave behind, you can look in the back, but I wouldn't do it unless you have to."

I really wanted to look in the back, but considering the things I'd already seen, I wouldn't. I lifted Shadia's hand and kissed it before I opened the front cover.

The notebook contained information on a variety of zombies. There were pictures marked with dates, sickness, day-number, then with notes on how the zombie had changed from one picture to the next.

The first was of a woman in her fifties. André had managed to take a picture of her just after she turned if I was to judge from the lack of rot on her face or blood between her teeth. She was dressed in a clean dress, and her red hair was braided. Someone had clearly cared for her after she died. In every picture, she had the same background, like she was stuck in a room, and André took pictures of her through a window. I watched as she rotted day by day until her yellow dress was stained by the liquids flowing from her body, and her earlier full face turned shaggy and empty. On day three, she had blood around her mouth, but it looked old. After that, she never seemed to have any fresh blood on her. By day fifteen, which was the last picture, she was on the floor, glaring up at the camera with black eyes.

I flipped through the rest of the book: it was filled with a multitude of other zombies. There were the ones stuck between the cars where André had found us, and some walking around the city with orange crosses painted on their faces. I remembered seeing those crosses, and when I looked up, André gave a small nod and lifted his hands, showing the orange paint stains I'd noticed before.

"So you watch the zombies, and then what?" I asked, closing the book when I came to a blank page.

He shrugged. "Try to solve the mystery. You saw that woman in the beginning, right? I've watched her every day since she turned, and if they aren't fed regularly, they decompose pretty much as a normal dead person would. You saw today's picture, right? She couldn't stand up anymore."

He'd finished his bierwurst while I looked through the book and was back to fiddling with his hair. He still wouldn't look at us.

"Thanks for letting me look," I said, handing the book back to him. My head felt heavy and tired, and all I wanted was to go back to sleep. I wanted to forget those pictures and the words written around them. I wanted not to know the things I now knew about the parasite. Just sleep and not remember.

"Do you have any idea how they find us?" Shadia asked, drawing me out of my thoughts.

"What do you mean?" André answered.

"They must be able to find us somehow, right? Do they smell us? Hear us? See us? Do you have any idea how their senses work?"

"No."

"Any chance they can smell blood?"

"Like sharks?" I asked.

Shadia nodded, not taking her eyes off of André. He was chewing on his bottom lip, his eyes unfocused.

"No," he finally answered. "Why?"

Shadia shrugged. "My period started yesterday. It would be a big inconvenience if they could track me because of it."

I snorted a laugh, both at her comment and at the blush exploding across André's cheeks.

"Well, no ... I don't ... that is ... don't think ... that's a problem, you know?" he stammered, not looking at either of us.

"Good," Shadia answered, smiling a half-smile at his discomfort.

For a few seconds, we sat there, André not looking at us and fidgeting as if he wanted to run from the room as fast as possible. Men and their fear of menstruation never ceased to amaze me.

Finally, André cleared his throat and forced himself to look at us. "There's one more thing."

"OK?" Shadia and I said in unison.

Still not looking at us, André pulled a smaller notebook from his bag and handed it to us. On the first page, he'd written 'Patient X', and below followed a short description. 'Male, mid-twenties, 178cm tall and 54kg heavy', I glanced up at André, estimating his weight and height, but Shadia was turning the page. Her sharp gasp made me look down again.

On the page was a bloody... something. The blood was fresh and red, and in-between, I could see small wounds in a half-moon shape. Under the picture, he had written: 'Day 0. The patient bit at 11:27 by subject 1, Old Woman'.

On the next page was another picture of the wound, but no blood. This time it was clear it was a bite mark from a human mouth, and from what little I could see in the picture, I guessed it was located where the shoulder met the neck.

'Day 1. No change'.

Each page after that had another picture of the wound, which had stopped bleeding but didn't seem to heal, and a small comment below with what day it was and changes in the patient. There didn't seem to be many, other than the pain subsiding.

All in all, there were nine pictures logged.

"This is you, isn't it?" Shadia asked. I couldn't tear my eyes away from the picture on the last page as she spoke. "You were bitten by one of them and have been logging your progress." It wasn't a question.

Finally, I looked up at André.

He didn't answer but unwound the scarf from around his neck. He dropped it to the ground, and I could see what looked like a red tattoo peeking out of his t-shirt before he pulled the neckline aside and showed us the wound. It was as fresh and clear as in the pictures.

12

"How could you?" Shadia yelled for the hundredth time. "How could you let us take this risk? What if you turned on us, huh? What would we have done then? You knew the risk when you brought us in here, and you didn't tell us."

"I've told you now," André answered, also for the hundredth time.

Shadia's feet stomped back and forth across the concrete floor as she yelled at André like he was a child.

"Why did you tell us now, then? Why didn't you just let Kit heal, and we'd be out of your hair?"

"Well, you know, I was wondering if I might come with you," André mumbled.

"What?" Shadia's shrill shriek made my ears burn. "Why would we take you with us? You're a ticking time bomb. Why should we take that risk?"

I opened my eyes for the first time since Shadia started yelling. "Sha," I said, and she appeared in the doorway. "Let him come."

Her mouth fell open. "What? Why?"

"Because we could use the extra help. We left home almost a week ago and aren't even out of the city. How're we gonna get to the cabin at this rate?" I locked my eyes with hers. "We won't. Not on our own. I'm slowing us down. I'm not saying you leave me behind," I hurried on when she clenched her jaw, "but I'm saying we bring him. Now we know he's been bitten. He hasn't turned in days. Maybe he won't turn at all. In which case, we have an extra pair of eyes and hands keeping us alive. If not, we deal with it when we need to." My voice grew in strength as I spoke, and I pushed up until I was leaning on my elbows.

Shadia stared at me for a long time before she sighed and turned, probably to look at André who was somewhere in the other room. "Fine. You can come. But I want the patient book. I want to take your daily picture and checks; you got me? You say nothing has changed, but there may be things you won't notice that I will."

"As long as you don't see those changes when they aren't there," I said, at the same time as André said: "Are you a doctor?"

"I won't, Kit," Shadia answered without turning away from André. "And no, but neither are you. I am, however, used to looking for symptoms and trying to figure them out." At this, her eyes wavered, almost jumping to me but not quite.

"Fine, that's settled," I said, pushing up into a full sitting position. "André, what about your other … subjects? What'll you do?" I wasn't sure what I meant by that. What could he do? Hunt around town for his zombies and kill them? Bring them with us?

The sound of his feet shuffling over the concrete preceded him as he arrived in the doorway. "If it's OK with the two of you, I want to check on them tomorrow; then we can leave the day after that?"

Exchanging a glance with Shadia, I nodded and fell back on the bed, regretting it the moment the impact sent a shock of pain through my back. Falling on concrete was not recommended.

"How were you bitten?" I asked.

André's ears turned red, and he looked away. "I tried to get close to the subject," he said in so low a voice I wasn't sure I'd heard right at first. "I... did an experiment, and it didn't work out."

"What kind of experiment?" Shadia asked.

André's hands clenched into fists. "Nothing important," he mumbled before he turned and marched off to the bathroom. Shadia and I exchanged a glance, and agreed without a word to drop it at that.

We spent hours packing. Or, Shadia and André packed, and I stayed in bed, pointing out what we might need and what we might not. Between André and my own fascination with apocalyptic shows before the actual apocalypse happened, we should be safe enough.

There was one messenger bag with medication alone; strong pain medication for me and weaker ones for the other two. There were antibiotics and antibacterial sprays and gels. Bandages and band-aids and everything else one could think to have in a medical bag. This bag would stay with me at all times. As Shadia pointed out, it was the one bag we couldn't afford to lose, and she would not leave me behind, so if I wore it, it would make it with us. Neither of us argued. We also put in a few other essentials, just in case I got separated from the others somehow.

There was another bag with canned foods, and another with just water. That one would travel on the back of my chair, making it a little easier for us to carry. We'd tested it on the chair yesterday, and while it was heavy, it was easier than actually carrying it.

We didn't talk any more about André being bitten or his experiments, but it hung over us all like a dark cloud. It was a relief when we were done and went to our separate rooms.

The next morning, Shadia woke early, waking me with her so I could watch as she checked out André's wound, just in case. It was a quick and easy affair. She photographed the wound, which still hadn't started to heal, and took his temperature and pulse. She was a lot more thorough with her checks than he had been, even asking if he'd noticed any blood in his waste. He blushed and stammered a 'no', and hurried to leave for the daily check on his zombies.

"What if he doesn't come back? I wouldn't after questions like that," I said as I lay back on the bed.

Shadia shrugged. "Then we leave without him."

She started preparing breakfast. The two of us would have run out of food by now, but André had a big stash of canned goods, bottled water, and medication. He even had a sun-charger for phones and other electronics, including Shadia's Kindle. It looked like he'd raided every shop and pharmacy on this side of town. We couldn't bring even half of it with us, but at least we knew we would have more than enough supplies for a while. The fact that we wouldn't have to worry about finding more medication before reaching the cabin was a great load off my shoulders. Even Shadia seemed lighter knowing that.

Shadia and I spent the rest of the day relaxing and talking, discussing the plan. André had a map, and we'd drawn out the best way for us to get to the freeway and the road beside it. He agreed that was the best course of action we could take. The only thing he mentioned was trying to avoid the cult in the park. There was no telling what they would do if they saw a guy and two women walking along. Or, well, one of the women walking and one in a chair, which was another thing he was concerned about. If they were so obsessed with health, how would they react to me? For now, all we had to do was wait for him to return, and the night to turn to day.

I joked with Shadia that there were many adult things we could do to pass the time, but she shot that down quickly. I wasn't surprised, so I snuggled into her arms, happy with the cuddles.

"What do we do if we get split up?" I asked after a while.

It took so long for Shadia to answer, I thought she might have fallen asleep, but finally, she said: "Then we meet up again."

I sat up to look at her. "How?"

She pulled me down to lie on her again. "The train stations," she said when I was comfortable. "If we get split up, we both go to the next train station and wait for the other there."

I opened my mouth to ask how long we should wait. What if the other one didn't come? What would we do then? But Shadia shushed me before I was able to form the words, and I closed my mouth again. It was nothing to worry about, because it wouldn't happen. We would stay together, and we would be safe.

André returned and hurried into his room. There was black blood on his hands, and he smelled of fear and wet iron. We didn't bother him as he cleaned up and got himself put together. When he reemerged, there was no sign of the wild look he had worn when he entered. Shadia checked his wound again and did the whole routine anew before they prepared dinner.

We went to bed early that night and woke even earlier. It was time to hit the road again.

13

"Well, there was no sign of any cancer on the tests, Katerina," the doctor said, turning away from his computer to look at me.

"OK, so why do I feel sick?" I answered, clenching my hands in my lap.

The doctor sighed. "Well, it isn't unusual for the body to react badly to chemotherapy. We pump you full of poison, after all, and that has some effect."

"Not a year after the last treatment, it shouldn't," Shadia said from beside me. Her hands were folded in her lap as well, but more out of anger than fear. Her face was angry as well. Jaw set, barely moving to speak, and eyes hard as they stared at the doctor. "She should at least be able to work a little by now. It's been a year."

"Speaking of which," the doctor said, turning a little in his chair to look at the screen again, "why aren't you working? You should be back to at least fifty percent by now."

Shadia opened her mouth to speak, but I reached over and took her hand. "I'm not working 'cause when I tried twenty percent half a year ago, I passed out the first day. When I tried again the week after, I threw up before one hour had passed."

"What do you work with?"

"Packaging in storage."

"OK. So why didn't you try any more than those two times?"

"Because you said she needed more time," Shadia growled.

"It may just be that your body needs a kick. Have you tried working out?"

"Yes," I answered, not able to keep the anger from my voice this time. "Three months ago, when you suggested it. I tried joining Shadia for a walk and ended up bedbound for four days, too weak to even dress myself."

The doctor pursed his lips. "Well, that's not good."

"No, it is not," Shadia said. "So what is going on with her? Why is she like this?"

"I don't know."

"What can we do about it?" I asked, squeezing Shadia's hand to keep her from blowing up.

"I'll order some new tests. We'll figure this out, don't worry."

But I was worried. He'd almost missed my cancer when I came to him two years ago. He hadn't believed me about my failing health after the treatment ended. I'd had to trick him into taking blood last time I was here. This was the first time he'd even considered that something else could be going on. I was worried, because my body didn't feel right.

Voices woke me. When I looked up, I saw Shadia was examining André's wound again. When he saw me looking, he rolled his eyes to try and hide a blush. I hid my smile and sat up, stretching. As André started pulling his shirt back on, I noticed he was sweating a little. Was he nervous about leaving? I was ready to move out of this basement and get on the road again.

Shadia didn't let it happen as fast as André or I wanted, however. She forced us both to eat something, as well as talk about our route and what to do if we got separated. She also forced us to look at the map so we would know roughly where the train stations were.

Finally, we were ready.

André headed up the stairs first, to make sure there were no zombies waiting to get in our way. He returned with a thumbs up before he grabbed my chair and started dragging it up the stairs. He'd practiced folding it in and out again a million times yesterday so he could do it on the run if he had to. When he returned the second time, he grabbed the extra bags and carried them up the stairs as well. On his third descent, it was my turn.

Shadia and André had discussed how best to make sure I stayed with them. We would all be dragging a lot of stuff with us, so for Shadia to carry me on her back wouldn't work for long. In case we were chased by zombies and came to an area where we had to leave the chair, we needed a plan B. André, the little scavenger that he was, had an idea. He'd seen rescuers use a foldable kind of stretcher, and so he'd sat up last night to make one. It was just a sheet, strong ropes, and two metal pipes, but it was easy to fold together and put in a bag. It was not comfortable to lie on, but who was I to complain?

The trip up the stairs was a bumpy one, but at least we got to the top where they lowered me to the floor. Shadia helped me into the chair, and I turned to look out the big windows and onto the street as the others pulled on their bags and rucksacks. Everything looked quiet. No zombies walking around, hardly even any wind, but the hairs on my neck stood up anyway. It felt like someone was watching us.

"Here," André said, handing me a dark green bandana that almost matched my hair. Shadia was holding a purple one.

82

"What's that for?" I asked, taking it even as I spoke the words.

Before he answered, André pulled his own red bandana over his mouth and nose. "The smell," he said.

I tied the bandana around my throat and pulled it up. I was wearing my sunglasses and they fogged up at my first exhale.

"This'll be a problem," I murmured and tried to move the bandana away from the edge of the glasses.

"It's not like you need to see where you're going," Shadia said.

Before I could answer, she grabbed my hand and kissed my fingertips. I pulled down the bandana and stuck my tongue out at her before I pulled it back into place.

"You two ready?" André asked.

He'd walked to the doors and was staring through the glass onto the street. Or I thought he was watching the street, but when I turned his way, I saw he was looking up.

Shadia answered in the affirmative and moved to stand behind me, pushing me past the different gym machines and toward the door. André unlocked the chain holding the doors together—I couldn't help but wonder at the point when the doors were glass and most of the walls were glass, and it would be so easy to break in—and let it fall to the floor with a clatter that made my teeth itch.

The smell hit us first. It had been bad when we left our apartment days ago, but now it was like a blanket in the air. I could almost feel it against my skin and taste it in my mouth, lying like a layer on my tongue. Behind me, Shadia gagged audibly. I wasn't as loud, but I was also fighting against the muscles in my stomach that wanted to chuck up my breakfast.

André tapped the side of his nose, or his bandana, and winked at us before he stood aside to give us room. I considered popping a piece of gum in my mouth to try and fight the smell, but I was afraid it would only taste like death.

When she was done gagging, Shadia tipped me back to get me over the step, and we emerged into bright sunlight.

I blinked, blinded for a second, and by the hiss from behind, Shadia was the same. My eyes closed, I heard the echo of a dead moan from somewhere behind me, too low to be any threat. Then I heard something else: boots on asphalt.

My eyes blinked open. It was still too bright for me to see anything clearly, but I heard how Shadia drew in a gasp, and André cursed. Then, a new voice spoke:

"What a nice surprise."

14

"Who are you?" the voice of an adult man asked.

My eyes blinked into focus at the words. I guessed the owner of the voice was the man standing right in front of us. He was tall and well built, but with a gaunt look to his face that reminded me of sickness. He stood in the middle of the road, in-between cars, and I guess he had hidden there until André was done bringing stuff up. How long had he waited? There were two men standing beside him, and two more were walking toward us along the sidewalk, one to either side. All the men were wearing bandanas or scarves around their faces, just like us.

"Who're you?" I asked, trying to meet his eyes before I realized he wouldn't see mine behind the glasses. He wasn't really looking at me anyway. He barely seemed to register that I was part of the group. His eyes were on Shadia, running up and down her fit body.

"She asked you a question," Shadia said.

"How rude of me not to introduce myself," the man answered, and walked past the car standing between him and us. The two men beside him stayed put, but the ones on the sidewalk were only meters away now. They stopped there. "My name is Nicholas Glass. And you?"

"My name is Shadia, this is André," she gestured to his cringing form. He was almost hiding behind us, and I couldn't say I blamed him. Something about Nicholas was overpowering. "And this is my wife, Kit." Shadia squeezed my shoulder. At the word 'wife', Nicholas finally looked down at me, his nose wrinkling.

"I hope you don't think me rude, but I did not expect to see anyone like you again," he said, his voice as hard as a rock.

"I do," I answered, looking up at him but doing my best to look down at him at the same time.

His brow furrowed in confusion. "Do what?"

"Think you rude." He opened his mouth, but I continued before he could defend himself. "But I'll forgive you. It's a natural thought to have, with the state of the world and all." Shadia squeezed my shoulder again, but I wasn't sure if she was asking me to be careful or egging me on. "Nice to meet you, Nicholas," I finished, putting out my hand. I did not want to shake his hand–who knew what kind of germs he was carrying around–but I'd long since learned that the only way to deal with ableist people was to face them head-on. Force them to see me as an equal by acting as if it was my right. It was, but they didn't see it that way.

He stared at the hand for a heartbeat before he took it, giving one quick shake and letting go, then returning his gaze to Shadia. There was something hungry in his eyes that I didn't like.

"I have to agree with my girl, Nicholas. And if you don't mind, we have a fair distance to go before lunch and should really be on our way," Shadia said, taking her hand off my shoulder. I guessed she returned it to the handle behind me, ready to move if we needed to.

"Oh? And where would you be going?"

"To a family cabin."

"Why?"

"Because it's safe."

The man to our right coughed, and we all turned to look at him. "There's nowhere safe now," he said, his eyes sad in contrast to his rough voice.

"Nowhere but here," Nicholas said. "We have a safe place."

"I bet," I murmured, but no one seemed to hear.

"And where is that?" Shadia asked, sounding bored.

"Vigeland Parken, of course! We have a small village there, and you know what they say about villages." Nicholas winked.

"Uhm, I don't," André said, finally speaking up.

Nicholas's smile faltered. "That it takes a village."

"To do what?"

I snorted a laugh and heard two of the men do the same.

"To … do stuff," Nicholas said, clearly unsure. Then he cleared his throat and continued, back in character. "To survive, in this case."

"It is nice of you to offer," Shadia said, bringing the attention back to her. "I assume you're offering to bring us to your safe haven, your village? Why else mention it?"

"That is correct."

"But, as I said, we know somewhere safe and will be going there instead."

Nicholas's smile fell. "That is mighty rude of you."

"Why?"

He spread his arms. "Here we are, offering you safety and sanctuary, and you throw it back in our faces?"

"I'm not throwing anything. Just saying 'no thank you' to an offer, as you just called it. That is my right, is it not?"

"There are no rights or wrongs anymore," Nicholas said, his eyes going dark.

"Let's just go," I said, bringing his eyes to me again.

"Yeah," André said, barely loud enough for us to hear. "We should go."

"I think we should. Good luck with your village, Nicholas." Shadia's voice was all steel and professionalism as she turned my chair around and started walking.

"Well, then I think we have a problem," Nicholas said from behind us. Shadia didn't stop but sped up a little. I wasn't sure anyone other than me noticed. "You see, we are trying to save the human race, and letting possible mothers go, goes against everything we stand for."

We reached the man on our side. For a second, I thought he would step away and let us pass, but at the last moment, he stepped into me. My chair whipped to the side, and Shadia lost her grip. I banged into a car. The metal against metal screamed as the chair tipped and I was thrown to the asphalt. Shadia yelled my name and bent to help me up, but the man grabbed her and threw his arms around her, holding her in place.

"What the hell do you think you're doing?!" Shadia screamed as she kicked and bucked, trying to get loose.

André rushed forward, trying to pry the man's arms off her, but the others were there in an instant. Grabbing him, they pushed him against the stone wall until he grunted with pain.

I pushed up and crawled toward Shadia. One hand gripping my ax, I pulled down my bandana and growled at the man holding her.

A boot fell on the hand holding the ax, pushing it into the asphalt and grinding until I had to splay my fingers or they would be crushed. Gritting my teeth in pain, I looked up at Nicholas. Shadia was screaming my name.

"Now, now," Nicholas said, crouching so we were almost eye-to-eye. "What chance do you think someone like you stands against us?" He spread his arms to encompass the other men.

I spit, the glob hitting him just below the right eye.

His hand swung, hitting my cheek so hard I was flung to the side. I would have hit my head if not for my broad-brimmed hat taking most of the fall.

"Stupid girl," he snarled. Standing, he wiped the spit with the sleeve of his shirt. "I was going to bring you as well. While damaged, there might be something we could do with you. But now, you've ruined your chances."

He lifted his boot from my hand, and I hissed as a new kind of pain flared through me, making my fingers spasm with the sudden release.

"You sure, Nick?" one of the other men asked. "Don't you think she'll be a problem?"

Nicholas laughed. "Look at her. What kind of problem could she be?" He spat at me, but his aim was off.

"You'd be surprised," I said, showing my teeth in a growl before I flung myself forward. Grabbing his leg with both hands, I sunk my teeth into his naked calf. Blood exploded in my mouth, and I had to fight to not let go and throw up.

Nicholas was screaming, Shadia was screaming, the other men were screaming. Someone grabbed me and tried to pull me away, but I just dug in deeper, not letting go, even as blood flooded my mouth and poured down my chin. Yuck, yuck, yuck! But no way was I letting this man take Shadia from me. No way. Someone grabbed my hair, and the sudden pain made me yelp, letting go. The owner of the hand yanked me back as Nicholas started crawling backwards away from me. I kicked at the one holding me, hitting something soft that made him grunt in pain.

"You let her go!" I snarled and wriggled out of the grip before crawling toward Nicholas again. "You let Shadia go right now, or I swear, I'll bite off more than a piece of flesh."

I gripped his leg, slick with blood, and crawled up him, my fingers digging into his skin. He was screaming nonsense, his eyes wide with pain and fear.

"OK," the man holding Shadia said, letting her go. "OK, we'll let you go."

Shadia hurtled from his arms and toward me, grabbing me and pulling me away from Nicholas.

"And André," I said, turning my eyes and snarl on the man that had spoken. "You let us all go."

"Of course," he answered, gesturing at the two holding André.

They let him go and moved toward Nicholas, but stopped far enough away that I couldn't reach them. Shadia was murmuring in my ear, begging me to let go and come with her. I let her drag me toward the chair that André was turning the right way up and rolled toward us, my ax in his hands. I was in the seat before I even knew it, and André was pushing me forward as Shadia walked at my side, holding my hand and keeping her eyes on the men. They were glaring at us, all except Nicholas, who was still screaming and staring at his leg. I couldn't help but smile at the sight, and the two youngest men looked away, turning pale.

"What were you thinking?" Shadia hissed as we neared the end of the street.

"Mostly yuck," I answered, using my gloves to wipe the blood from around my mouth.

"Katerina," the warning in Shadia's tone wasn't to be mistaken.

"I wasn't thinking at all," I said, looking up at her. "Just that I couldn't let them take you."

Her hand tightened around mine.

We reached the end of the street.

"No matter what you were thinking, you got us out of that, you know, and now I think we need to get out of here before they decide to follow," André said, looking back at the men.

We followed his gaze. They'd managed to pull Nicholas to his feet. The wounded man seemed to have come to his senses. I could almost feel his eyes burning holes in me.

"Good idea," Shadia said and turned toward the road.

15

After the street we were on, the next would be one of the main roads through town, and that would bring us to the freeway and the small road beside it. We didn't dare take our time, though. Having left Nicholas behind, wounded, it felt like it would only be so long before he sent men after us. For one, as he'd said himself, he didn't want to let a possible mother go. For two, he struck me as the kind of guy that didn't like to be made a fool off. Especially by someone he saw as inferior to himself, AKA me.

Bygdøy Allé was, as we'd expected from the map, the next street down, but we were on the wrong side from where we needed to go, so again I had to crawl onto Shadia's back and let her carry me past the cars.

We were halfway across the street when I saw it. "Wait," I said. "You see that?" I pointed with the ax at the person coming toward us.

Shadia nodded. "Just one. We can deal with that."

I opened my mouth to argue but closed it again.

Across the street, Shadia lowered me to sit on the hood of a car, then walked on, pulling the knife from her belt. I looked away, focusing on getting myself into the chair. By the time I looked up again, Shadia was pushing its body to the side so it wouldn't be in the way of my wheels. As I was rolled past, I couldn't help but look at the body. Once a man, it was now shriveled, barely a husk of what it must have been. Dressed in just it's boxers, it looked pitiable.

"There!"

It wasn't loud, just enough for me to hear over the sounds of my chair, my breathing, and André's panting, but I did hear it. The yell made my head shoot up, and I turned in the chair. It came from one of the men that had been with Nicholas. He and one other stood at the end of the road, pointing at us.

"OK, we have to hurry up now," I said, my voice a little too high.

Shadia heard me and turned. Her eyes jumped from me to the men, then to André. "When we get across that next street, I'm taking her," she said matter of factly. André nodded, concentrating on breathing.

We reached the next road. Shadia stood almost before I was on her back, marching across without a glance back.

As soon as we were on the other side, she hurried back to André. He was almost across the road, managing my folded up chair as best he could, panting and sweating and really not looking good. Despite being thin as a reed, I guessed he hadn't worked out much before the zompocalypse.

As I waited, I pushed a stick of gum into my mouth. It tasted of blood, but I forced myself to chew until cranberry filled my mouth. I couldn't hear what Shadia was saying to André, but I saw him drink the rest of his water bottle before he pulled a bierwurst from his rucksack and started chewing on it as he followed Shadia, pushing the chair across the road.

Without a word, she helped me into the chair and we continued onward. The pace was a little faster now that André could focus just on himself. Despite him eating as he moved, he was walking faster than before. I couldn't picture eating at such a time, but he did what he thought was best.

I turned to look behind us, seeing the two men moving toward us but at a slower pace than I would have expected. Why weren't they chasing us with everything they had? They could overtake us if they tried.

We reached another intersection, this one bigger than the others. André's breathing was better, and he'd finished eating his sausage. Shadia squatted before me again, and I climbed onto her back. This time, though, she stayed and made sure that André got the chair folded up right before she moved on.

There had been an accident here. Two cars had driven into each other, nose to nose, and others had crashed into both of them on their respective sides, pushing them around. It looked like three other cars had been involved in the accident as well, with crushed fronts or sides.

Shadia squeezed between one of the crushed cars and one that had just managed not to hit it. Her face was turned upward, looking forward, so she didn't see the body inside the car. It was a pregnant woman. Dark, dried blood covered her face. The body of a toddler sat in the back seat, strapped in. As I looked, it turned its head and stared at me with black eyes. It opened its mouth and clacked its small, white teeth together as it reached for me.

I turned away, biting my lower lip to keep from crying and thanked the stars that Shadia hadn't seen the baby. After the kids at the school, this would destroy her. Still, I couldn't help but wonder how the baby had turned. Had it been sick already when the crash happened but not been killed by the accident? Left to die of the sickness? I would have to ask

André if he thought the parasite could still take over if the body died before it had completed its growth. How sick must the baby, the mom, have been as they tried to escape the city for this to happen?

André seemed better as he unfolded the chair, but he kept glancing over his shoulder at the two men following us. The accident was the only thing between us now.

I almost fell into the chair as Shadia let me go and hurried to stand behind me. Before I was even properly in place, she was moving at a fast jog. One of the men raised his voice behind us. I looked back and saw that they had sped up.

"André," Shadia said, and I saw him come up beside her. His mouth was gaping as he breathed, but he didn't seem too tired, thankfully. "Run ahead and see if there are any cars we can use."

"What?" he panted.

"There might be a car or two with the key still in them standing on the ramp. We need to move fast to get away from those guys, and we can't move all that fast as things are."

"Oh, right. OK, I'll try."

He pushed past. He wasn't much faster than Shadia, but fast enough that by the time we reached the on-ramp to the freeway, he was nearly at the top. The cars weren't as piled up here, so Shadia managed to maneuver me in the chair between the cars and onto the ramp. As we turned past another car, I turned and saw the two men weren't far behind.

"Sha, we have to hurry," I murmured, not wanting to stress her but not sure what else to do.

"I know, *habibi*," she said, her voice a little strained, but she didn't slow.

We were on the bridge, running along the outer edge to

avoid cars. Ahead, André was gone from sight, but I could hear him cursing. Behind, the men were on the bridge as well, speeding up now that there was nothing in their way.

I heard their steps too close a second before one of them came from the side, grabbing for Shadia's ponytail. Shadia ducked and spun, letting me go as she did. Her hand flew out, knit in a fist, and right into the man's solar plexus, knocking the breath from him and pushing him back into his buddy.

I was just aware enough to stop myself from driving into a car, but even before I had time to right myself, Shadia was there again, grabbing me and pushing me through the throng of vehicles.

The men were cursing, or the man with breath enough was cursing, and trying to get to their feet, but they were tangled in each other. That delay was all we needed.

From ahead came the sound of a car starting up and a triumphant howl from André. I couldn't help but howl back as we passed the last car between him and us.

It was an old Volkswagen Polo, dirty yellow and too small for us, but right now we couldn't be picky. André had left the doors open and was opening the back to throw in his bags as we reached him.

Shadia called out just seconds before she let me go, and I gripped the wheels, feeling them bite into the gloves but not burning me. Shadia sprinted past, throwing her own bag to André and turning toward me again, reaching for the bags hanging on the back of my chair. In answer, I turned on one of my brakes, so I spun around, giving her my back. This made me look toward our stalkers, now on their feet and getting closer.

My hand was aching from where Nicholas had stepped on it,

and I could still taste his blood, even though I'd been spitting and chewing. I wanted to puke but felt kind of numb. That reminder was what made me lift the ax and scream wordlessly at the two men.

They faltered at the sound, glancing at each other.

"What the hell do you want?" I growled at them. "Why can't you just leave us alone?"

The oldest man, the one who had let Shadia go, shook his head. "We can't. Or rather, we can let you go," he pointed from me to Shadia, "but not her. We need every abled body woman left alive to fulfill our destiny." As he spoke, his voice grew stronger and he took another step toward us. "It is our sacred duty."

I whistled. "Wow, André was right. You're a cult." The man blinked. "But we don't share your beliefs," I hefted my ax as they both took a step forward. "And if you take one more step, I'll use this on you."

The men stared at me for a long time, not moving. Nothing happened for a heartbeat. I could feel sweat building on my neck, and tears flowed from my eyes as a result of the light.

"This is stupid," the youngest of the men said and rushed forward.

His sudden movement made my tense muscles react on instinct, and I swung. The blade bit into his upper arm and blood splattered the side of the car as he was thrown off his feet with a yowl of pain.

I pulled the ax from his arm before I completely understood what I had done. He was screaming and screaming, clutching at his almost severed arm. The older man had run to his side and was trying to stop the bleeding, forgetting about us.

"Kit," Shadia hissed and pulled the ax from my hands. "Come

on. This is our chance."

I didn't argue, didn't do anything, as she pulled me out of the chair and into the back of the car. André was there in a second, folding up the wheelchair and closing the car door behind us.

As soon as she was sure I was secure across the seats, Shadia pulled the front seat back into place and crawled into it, pulling on her seatbelt as she checked that the mirror was correctly placed. André jumped into the passenger seat, and Shadia revved the engine.

She backed up as André closed his door, made a sharp turn, and shot down the open road.

I lifted myself and looked through the backwindow to see the two men on the ground. The older guy now shirtless as he tried to tie up the other man's arm. There was blood everywhere.

"*Habibi*, don't watch," Shadia said, her voice shrill in my ears.

I turned to the front and stared at her in the rear-view mirror. The taste of blood was still in my mouth, the now-dead gum growing too big to chew. I looked down at the bloody ax lying on the floor of the car. There were no windows to open in the back of the small Polo, so I threw up in an old McDonald's bag.

Excerpt from Medical Notebook

The parasite, for it turned out to be a living organism causing this, went undetected for a long time. It isn't the worm in itself that kills, but the eggs flooding the system, clogging the brain. But it is the worm that keeps the subject from dying. Or returning from the dead; however, you want to say it.

When it hatches, it eats its way through flesh and into your stomach. There, it integrates itself into the stomach wall and starts stealing food. It only eats meat.

The worm lay eggs through the same hole through which it eats, and so the stomach is soon filled with eggs that move through the body before being expelled, increasing the host's hunger. Especially for meat, as the body no longer receives the expected nutrients. When expelled, they can spread, and they spread fast.

16

The slowing of the car woke me. I didn't know when or how I'd fallen asleep between the reek of vomit, the taste of it in my mouth, and the tears that wouldn't stop running from my eyes. I'd used a whole packet of gum to take the taste away, as well as way too many antibacterial napkins to clean my hands and face, removing every trace of blood I could find.

But I had fallen asleep, and now the car smelled a little less of vomit.

"Why're you stopping?" I asked as I blinked my eyes open.

The sunlight hadn't changed much while I slept, and my cheeks still felt raw from crying, so I couldn't have slept for more than half an hour at the most.

"The road is blocked," Shadia said, stopping the car completely.

I sat up and looked out the window. There were fields as far as I could see, with pockets of forest and homes here and there. The road in front of us, however, was completely blocked by cars. There weren't as many as back in Oslo, but it was clear there had been an accident, and people had left their cars behind.

"Where are we?" I asked.

"I honestly don't know, but not far past Ikea."

Closing my eyes, I mentally called up the map we'd looked at yesterday. "That's not far at all."

"No, but it's given us a head start in case Nicholas wants to follow. There don't seem to be that many zombies out here either. We've passed three since Ikea."

"That sounds like plenty to me."

Shadia shook her head. "Not if you'd seen how many we passed before, *habibi*. They came in packs. I guess they all died at one of the centers and somehow got out." She turned and looked out the back window.

I turned to look with her, but the road was empty. "I'm afraid they're following us anyway," I said.

"They will get distracted."

I nodded and swallowed hard a couple of times before I was able to look at her face. Beside her, I saw André. He was curled into the smallest ball he could be, back toward us and head leaning against the window. His breathing was uneven but slow.

Shadia followed my look with her own and gave a small squeeze of my hand. "He fell asleep almost as soon as you did. I guess it was too much for both of you."

"What about you?" I asked. "How're you doing?"

Shadia smiled, but it didn't reach her eyes. "Better than the two of you, I'm sure." I stuck my tongue out at her, trying to make her smile. It didn't work. "But I don't feel safe just sitting here. We should get a move on."

"So, what's the plan now?"

"We have three choices." She held up the three middle fingers on her hand. "One, we try to move the cars." She lowered one finger. "Two, we go off-road." She pointed her second finger in the air.

"Oh, wait!" I said as she opened her mouth to speak. She closed it again and blinked at me. Tongue between my teeth, I reached forward and fiddled with her hand until her middle finger was the only one sticking into the air. "There!"

Shadia rolled her eyes. "Real mature, *habibi*."

"You love me." The banter worked much better than my grimace to make Shadia relax.

She rolled her eyes yet again, this time smiling, before she became serious once again. "Or three, we walk and find a place to rest for the day."

"You think we need rest already?"

She furrowed her brow. "It depends on you and André."

"Should we wake him?"

"Probably?"

When Shadia didn't do anything, I leaned forward and poked André. Shadia was still holding the other. He groaned in his sleep, so I poked him again. This time, he swatted at my hand, and I poked a third time.

"What?" he snapped, finally uncurling from his ball and turning to scowl at me. His eyes were shiny as if he had a fever, and his skin was clammy with sweat.

Worry coiled in my stomach, and I glanced at Shadia. By the furrow of her brow, she was worried as well.

"We're stuck," I said matter of fact.

His scowl turned into a frown. "Where are we?"

I let Shadia fill him in as I stretched my back and neck. They'd knotted up while I slept and cracked like fireworks now. Shadia winched with every pop, and André looked at me with big eyes, seeming impressed.

"Well, I don't think we can move those cars. And I don't

think we can go off-road, you know?" he said when Shadia had given him our choices. "So, I guess we should walk?"

"Are you sure?" Shadia said, finally reaching for his forehead. "You don't look too good."

"I'm fine," he answered, dodging her hand so she couldn't get a proper feel of his temperature. "I'm just a little stressed after everything. I'm not good with stress, you know?"

Shadia and I exchanged glances before she nodded. "OK. So we start walking and keep our eyes open for any car that may have the keys close by."

"Maybe we could break into a house and steal the keys?" I wondered aloud.

Shadia scowled. "Kit, how could you say something like that?"

"What? It's not like the owners will be needing the keys or the car anytime soon."

"You don't know that."

"Actually, she has a point," André said in a low voice, afraid to get in the middle but clearly wanting to have his say. Not that I blamed him. His life was intertwined with ours whether he wanted it or not. "We don't know if the owners died in there or not. If we break into a house, we may end up letting a whole lot of zombies out. I still don't think their bite is contagious," he said in a hurry as Shadia opened her mouth. "But I don't want us to be eaten either, you know?"

Shadia sighed and rubbed the bridge of her nose. "OK," she finally said, throwing her hands in the air and slamming them into the ceiling of the small car. Grimacing, she continued. "We'll hit the road and keep our eyes open for any cars. If we pass a house with a car in the drive, we'll consider breaking in to get the keys. But only consider. Understood?"

"Yes, Mom," I said.

Shadia gave me a hard look that could actually have rivaled my mother's before she unbuckled her belt and climbed out of the car.

The thought of my mother stabbed at my heart, but I pushed it away. This was not a time for grief, but when was? I couldn't help but glance at Shadia, wondering how she was doing. The loss of my own family was painful, sure, but I had grieved losing them long ago. That's the thing with Myalgic Encephalomyelitis; you grieve the loss of your life and what that means.

Shadia, on the other hand, had a good relationship with her parents. They had met at school in Dubai, and her father had brought her mother home to Norway when they graduated. Shadia's whole family—her parents, grandparents, and two brothers—lived further North, and we lost contact with them a few days before things went bad in Oslo. She had spent a few days crying behind closed doors before we left, but she hadn't felled a tear or brought them up since then. Was she dealing, or in denial? Pushing through it?

"What about lunch?" André asked as he stepped out of the car, bringing me out of my thoughts.

17

We ate on the road. André stuck to his bierwursts while I ate canned peaches. I tried to talk André into eating something else, but he only grunted at me, and I let it go.

The fact that he was eating so much meat worried me. If the parasite lived on meat, wouldn't it be natural for it to crave more, and so make the host crave it? Or maybe he had loved bierwursts since before the shit hit the fan? What did I know? I wanted to talk to Shadia about it but didn't want to do it while André could hear, so I kept an eye on him, mulling it over.

Shadia didn't eat until André was done with his sausage, and he could take over pushing me. I felt a little bad for not being able to do it myself but shook it off just as fast. I would never quite be rid of that guilt, but I knew I couldn't do anything about it either, so feeling bad wouldn't help anyone.

The sun was warm, the asphalt mirroring the heat, and soon Shadia was walking with her jacket tied around her waist, sweat shining between her breasts every time I turned to talk to her. André was walking without his shoes and jacket, his pants rolled up. Every now and again, he would dance by me, the asphalt too hot for his naked feet. He was sweating as well, but in buckets compared to Shadia's glow. I did as André and rolled up my jeans and took off my jacket.

The landscape around us changed from small farms and fields to houses and gardens. Soon enough, we were surrounded by homes. I'd expected André to jump on the idea of us finding a car, but he was plowing along now, not even noticing the heat of the pavement beneath his feet. His eyes were unfocused, and he was panting.

"Maybe we should start looking for a place to sleep?" I offered, nudging my head toward André and hoping Shadia would notice and take my meaning.

"No," André answered before either of us could say anything else. "We need to get further before we stop for the day. You said it yourself, Shadia, those men might follow us, you know?" His voice was slurred like he'd been drinking.

Shadia let me go and moved toward him. "André, are you OK?"

He swatted her away as she reached for him. "I'm fine. Just tired and warm."

"We should get out of the sun."

"Not yet."

"Maybe we can look for a car?" I asked, rolling toward them. I could smell André from two meters away. A kind of sweetness. Shadia discreetly lifted her hand, asking me to stay back, so I did.

"That's not such a bad idea. We'll get further in a car and it will be cooler. What do you think, André? Will our luck hold once more?"

He shrugged. "How should I know?"

Shadia glanced at me before she shrugged as well. "Let's just start looking, OK? We should probably get something a little

106

bigger as well, so we have room for all of us and our things."

"Sure," he grumbled and shuffled forward again.

Shadia came to me and squeezed my shoulder.

"What're you thinking?" I asked, looking at her set jaw and furrowed brow.

"I'm worried, that's all."

"About the bite?"

"Yes."

I bit my lower lip for a second before speaking. "Do you think we should worry about him eating so much meat?"

The chair stuttered a little as Shadia slowed her pace. "Maybe. Maybe not. He might just like them." I nodded. "But we'll make a vegetable soup for dinner tonight, so he won't get any meat."

"Sounds good."

"You think we should be worried?"

I shrugged. "I don't know. He may just be stressed and having a reaction to everything that's happened today." I waved toward him, indicating his sweaty exterior.

Shadia shook her head, but not in denial. More like she tried to shake cobwebs off her thoughts. "Maybe. I hope so." She squeezed my shoulder again and moved to push me.

Our progress was slower after that. Part of it was looking for a car, but it was also because of André. He was dragging his feet more and more, leaning against cars as he looked at them, or using fences as support as he walked. I couldn't help but think about when I started having trouble with dizziness and my legs not wanting to listen early on in my sickness. How I would use everything as support, but not wanting to admit to anyone–even myself–that I needed it.

I asked André how he was feeling around half an hour later,

and he grunted for me to mind my own business. That he was fine but tired. I didn't argue, knowing too well how touchy one could be when not feeling well and not wanting to admit it.

We found an SUV that looked promising, but as Shadia neared its house, something hit the door from the inside. We all froze, listening, and the sound came again, and again, and again. Rhythmic and low. The thud of someone walking into the door repeatedly. After a short discussion, we didn't take the chance and moved on.

After another half hour, we finally found a car Shadia approved of. It was a Forester of some sort, big and bulky. I would probably eat through gas like there was no tomorrow, but it could hold all of us comfortably and looked good for off-road in case we had to drive through forests or fields to get past roadblocks. Who knew what the roads were like further South, after all. The only problem: there were no keys present.

"We could move on," I suggested, seeing Shadia eye the house it was parked beside.

"No. We could use the car. If only to get you both out of the sun so you don't burn. I'm surprised you haven't turned to ash by now," she answered, forcing a smile.

"What?" André asked as I said, "Harr harr."

"What?" he asked again as Shadia giggled.

"She's calling us vampires," I said, pointing between the two of us. "Sure, we're pale, but neither of us have fangs."

André narrowed his eyes at Shadia before giving a weak shrug like he didn't have the energy to complete it. "Well, someone did bite my neck."

Shadia's smile faltered, but I forced a laugh, recognizing black humor when I heard it. Shadia shot me a look before she shook her head and turned back to the house.

Drawing a deep breath, she headed for the door, ax in hand. She was almost there when a scrabbling sound from inside made her stop.

"Is that–" I began but was cut off by a muffled bark. "No," I breathed, pushing forward before I could even think about it.

"Kit," Shadia warned, seeing me from the corner of her eye.

"No," I answered. "We have to help it."

"It could be sick."

"But it isn't dead. Come on, Sha, I can't get to the door on my own."

Shadia sucked her bottom lip into her mouth, chewed on it once, then shook her entire upper body. Cursing in Arabic, she hurried up the steps to the door. The dog on the inside was whining now, having heard our voices.

"It's OK," I called in as calm a voice as I could. "We're here. We'll get you out."

It clawed at the door again.

Shadia knocked. "Hello? Is anyone in there?" The dog whined louder. Shadia knocked again, harder this time.

"It's alone," I said.

Shadia glanced at me before calling out again, just in case. "Shadia!"

Shadia glanced at me. "I'm afraid I'll hurt it."

"Aim high up," André said from beside me. I hadn't even noticed him following us. "Then, you can reach through and unlock the door, you know?"

Shadia nodded and hefted the ax. It bit into the wood with a crunch that made me shudder. The dog howled, and I wasn't sure if it was from fear or excitement.

Shadia made quick work of the door, hacking away the

upper half until she could look through. When she was sure nothing would jump out and bite her, she stuck her hand through the hole. Her lips were moving, but I couldn't hear any words. The lock clicked, and she dragged open the door, stepping back in case the dog flew out.

It didn't. Instead, it slunk into the sunlight.

"Oh, no," I whispered, tears filling my eyes.

It was a Border Collie, but its fur was tangled and tired. Even with that layer of dread-like fur, we could see its hip bones and ribs as it breathed. Its muzzle was covered in blood, and as it lifted its tail, I saw blood on its rear as well.

Shadia murmured something, maybe a prayer. I would have prayed as well if I believed in any gods.

The dog wagged its tail. It was a small wag, probably all it had the energy to do, but it was enough to spring the tears from my eyes as I leaned down.

"Here, little one," I said, reaching my hands out to it.

The dog's tail moved a little more as it walked clumsily down the steps. It looked at Shadia as it walked past, but didn't jump up or ask for any attention. I could see in its eyes that it was too tired to ask for anything. Reaching me, it sat down and rested its chin in my outstretched hand.

"Oh, dear one," I said, stroking its head and scratching behind its ears. "I'm so sorry."

"Kit," Shadia said as she headed down the steps.

"I know," I choked out, not taking my eyes off the dog, not breaking contact. The dog, hunched over as it was, too exhausted to even sit up properly, opened its mouth and panted. Its saliva was bloody, and I could smell vomit on its breath.

"It's infected," André said, his voice barely louder than a

breath.

"Yes, but you're still a good dog, aren't you?" The dog lifted a paw and rested it on my lower arm. "Shadia, give me your knife."

"*Habibi*, you don't–"

"I do."

Not breaking eye contact, or stopping my petting and scratching, I reached out the hand the dog had rested its chin on. It was leaning its head against my hand now, using me as support. For a moment, we jus sat there, then the dog tensed. It started gagging, and I just had time to push back before it threw up. There was no food in its vomit, only blood, and what looked like cloth.

I slid out of the chair, hitting the asphalt of the driveway with a thud that hurt my knees, and stroked the dog until it was done throwing up. It turned toward me again, looking miserable and tired.

"Here, little one. Rest," I said. When I had shuffled away from the vomit, I patted my thigh.

The dog blinked at me two times before following and lowering itself to the asphalt. Resting its head in my lap, it sighed and closed its eyes.

"Shadia," I said in a wobbly voice.

My tears dripped onto the dog's snout, but it didn't react. I could feel its heartbeat against my leg, slow and unsteady. It didn't have long.

Shadia, crying, took the knife from her belt and handed it to me. The moment I held it, she turned away, covering her mouth to stifle her sobs.

I didn't stop stroking the dog, didn't stop talking and telling it how good it was, that everything would be OK. I didn't stop crying, but I was able to keep it partly under control as I comforted. The knife in one hand, I waited.

It didn't take long. Half an hour, maybe. My legs were numb, and my face sore from the tears and the sun. Shadia was sitting behind me, her hand on my neck, giving silent support and comfort. André was sitting with his back against the car, eyes closed. He wasn't crying, but he kept swallowing hard, and his face was pale. Every now and again, he would look at the dog before hurriedly looking away. Then, the dog sighed again, and I felt its heartbeat stop against my leg. The starved body suddenly grew a lot heavier.

"There you go," I said, carefully reaching around to check the collar. Looking at the bone-shaped tag, I choked but swallowed the sob. "There you go, Max. You're safe now."

I stroked Max's head once more, just to make sure, then lined the knife up with his neck and pushed along the spine and into the skull.

18

André was the first to move. I wasn't sure how long he waited, but we sat so long that the blood flooding over my hands and legs cooled. Shadia sat behind me, arms wrapped around me as I sobbed.

André knelt beside me and touched my shoulder. His hand was shaking a little. "Kit," he began, voice hoarse and dry. Clearing his throat, he tried again. "We can't stay here, you know."

"Why not?" I whispered between sobs, not able to take my eyes off the dog.

"There are zombies on the way. Do you want them to get you?"

Shadia's arms tightened around me at his words. "How do you know?" she asked, her breath tickling my neck.

André sniffed. "Can't you smell 'em?"

Shadia sniffed. "Yes, I can."

I couldn't smell them, but I heard their moans. It was just at the edge of my hearing. I wouldn't have thought much about it if André hadn't pointed out they were coming closer. But even knowing this, I couldn't bring myself to move, to even look away from Max.

"We can't leave him," I finally said, fighting to hold back

another sob. "Not like this."

"*Habibi*," Shadia began, but I shook my head.

"No. We can't."

I could almost feel Shadia and André exchange glances behind my back.

"OK," Shadia finally said, kissing my neck. "We'll bury him, but first, we have to take care of the zombies, OK?"

"OK."

"And you can't just sit here while we do that. You have to defend yourself, OK?"

I nodded. Shadia squeezed me so tight I almost lost my breath before she stood. My hands shook as I dragged them through Max's fur one more time before letting her help me up and into my chair. For a second, I thought about all the blood I was dragging into the chair with me and how I would have to sit in it and remember this day forever, but I let the thought go. That wasn't important right now.

André bent and picked up Max. The dog had been huge in life and was probably even heavier now that he was all limp, but André staggered to his feet and wobbled his way to the small garden plot beside the driveway. My heart went out to him as I saw how his arms were shaking, and fresh sweat burst out on his forehead. André wasn't doing well, but he still thought about what would make me relax rather than what would be good for him. I wanted to do something for him in return, but I didn't know what.

We still had a little time before the zombies arrived, so while the others ate, I cleaned myself up. Again. My pink gloves seemed so dark I wasn't sure they could be saved, and that made my tears continue flowing. I wasn't sure I could stop them ever again.

Shadia made sure her shoulder touched my leg the entire time, letting me know she was there, and it was a small comfort.

It felt weird, just sitting there and waiting for the zombies to reach us, but right now, there wasn't that much else to do. Shadia stood for most of the talking while André was focused on keeping his food down and staying out of the sun. He was squinting against it as if it pained him. Every time it seemed Shadia considered asking how he was doing, he would switch the conversation over to something else, and I'd see the relief in his eyes that Shadia followed his lead and let him be. I'd done it myself many times to spare her the details of my pain, and it worried me that André felt the need to do it now.

Finally, the zombies came into view. There were only three, dressed in pajamas with blood on them. One was just a child.

Shadia let out a deep breath at the sight of the child zombie and turned toward one of the two adults. She gripped her knife, that I'd given back shortly after making sure Max wouldn't return, and headed forward. André glanced at the child, then at me, before he headed for the other adult, leaving the smaller zombie to me. I wondered why that was, and if it was really smart of André to go after one of the possibly stronger zombies with his body seeming as sick as it did, but I couldn't dwell on it for long.

The zombies all turned toward André, almost walking past Shadia, but she gripped the throat of her zombie and pushed it back.

André grabbed his zombie's shoulder and spun it around, making sure it saw only him. He let out a surprised yelp as the child zombie reached for him.

The sound woke me from my thoughts, and I hurried

forward. Pushing forward, I grabbed the ax with both hands and drove it into the side of the child zombie, pushing her away from André. I barely managed to keep her on her feet so she didn't go under my chair, and she hit the side of the car. Pinned between my ax and the vehicle, she clicked her teeth and reached for me.

OK, now what? How was I going to finish her off with my weapon, while using it to keep her in place?

To the side, Shadia felled her opponent and turned toward me.

I couldn't let Shadia kill a child, even if it was already dead. It would ruin her. But how could I kill it? I may not want kids of my own, but that didn't mean I hated or wanted to hurt them. Looking at the child in front of me, even as it clacked its teeth and tried to reach me, to hurt me, it was a child. Someone loved her, once. My eyes jumped from her mouth to her eyes. Those black eyes. Empty except for hunger. I'd made sure Max wouldn't come back like this, controlled by this thing, and I would release this child from its hold as well.

I pulled the ax toward me, gripping it with one hand. The child stumbled forward at the sudden release, almost falling to the ground, but I was close enough to support her. My hand was at her throat, holding her up, as I hefted the ax and brought it down on the zombie's head.

My eyes were locked on the child's black pits as the ax bit into her head and brain. As blood bubbled up around the blade, I saw the pupils retract, showing the child's usually bright blue irises.

With a hiccup, I let her go and watched as she crumbled to the asphalt. The ax slipped from her head as she fell, and I sat there, staring at her. What had I just seen? Had she still been in there? The essence of who she was? No. The bodies of the diseased were well and truly dead. If they returned, whatever once made them human was gone. I was sure of that. So what did it mean that the pupils returned to normal size as the body died? Was the parasite somehow looking through the eyes of its host?

"Kit!"

The call jarred me from my thoughts, and I spun around to locate the source. Shadia was sitting on the ground beside two bodies. One was André's zombie, spilling almost dried blood onto the ground. The other was André himself.

"What happened?" I asked and rolled closer. "Is he OK?"

"Do he look OK to you?" Shadia snapped. Her hand was at André's forehead, the other under his chin, making sure his airway was open. He had passed out.

"No," I answered meekly.

"Sorry," Shadia said. "I didn't mean to snap. I'm just scared."

She looked at me with big eyes, and all I could do was nod and say: "What do we do now?"

"We have to get him somewhere safe. Fast."

I looked around as Shadia made sure André was in a more comfortable position. His mouth was open, gasping for air, and his eyes were closed, but I could see his eyeballs moving under the lids. His skin was shining with sweat.

"He has a fever, doesn't he?" I asked. Shadia only nodded. "I think the easiest is to get him into the house. The door is already open, and nothing else has come out of it. We'd be safe there."

Shadia nodded again. "OK. André? Can you hear me?"

There was no response. No reaction.

Shadia sighed.

"Here," I said and slid out of my chair. My legs and arms were filled with lactic acid, but I didn't care. There were more important things to worry about. "Get him into my chair and up the stairs. It's easier than carrying him."

"You sure?"

I patted the ax. "I can take care of myself if I have to."

This only made the furrow in Shadia's brow deeper. Finally, she nodded and helped me to the side.

It was a battle for her to get André into the chair. While he was skinny, he was also completely limp and slippery, and he almost fell out of the chair on more than one occasion. But finally, he was in place, and Shadia leaned on the back of the chair to catch her breath. After a nod from me, she went to the stairs leading up to the door. I stared at the line of blood trailing after one of my chair's wheels as she moved, not able to look at André.

Shadia had to drag the chair up backwards, but she'd done it before, and I knew she had it under control. Instead of watching, I turned my attention to the street. The scent of the three zombies we'd already taken down was strong enough to mask the scent of any others coming our way. I hoped I would be able to hear them, as with the sun in my eyes I wasn't sure I'd see them.

It took Shadia a long time before she came out again, my empty chair in tow. She looked greyer, somehow. Her usually bouncy, dark hair looked flat, and her warm skin looked ashen.

"André?" I asked, not sure what to expect.

"In bed. Come on." Shadia helped me into the chair and pulled me toward the house. "It smells pretty bad. The dog ... he did his business inside for days, and there's ... there's death inside."

I only nodded and let her pull me up the steps and into the house. The scent of rotting flesh and sick dog hit me like a sledgehammer, and my vision swam, but the door had been open long enough to let some fresh air into the otherwise stale house, and I felt a draft. Shadia must have opened some windows.

The stairs to the second floor were just inside the doorway, and Shadia started pulling me up. As we moved, I looked at the pictures on the wall. A man and a woman. The woman and Max, the dog. Some family photos. Two teen boys, one goth and one jock. The teens and Max. The teens and the two adults. Then we were up the stairs, and Shadia rolled me to an open door.

The room on the inside held a double bed with a cover over the two duvets and pillows. Shadia kept it on as she put our bags on it and rolled me out again.

"Where are we going? Where's André?"

"We're getting you washed up, *habibi*. I won't let you crawl into a clean bed covered in blood." I couldn't argue with that. "And André is in another room, on a sofa. He needs a bath as well, but I'm hoping he'll wake up and take care of it himself soon. If not, I'll have to do it." When I turned to look at her, she shuddered theatrically, but her eyes and voice were empty. "I'm a lesbian for a reason. Now, let's get all that blood off of you."

19

I didn't see André again that day. He slept while I was awake and woke when I slept. Shadia told me she'd got him to eat something and clean up what she hadn't dealt with during the night.

After breakfast the next day, Shadia rolled me into André's room. It looked out over the garden where we'd left Max the day before. Sitting at the window, I watched as Shadia dug a hole in the ground. I argued that it was too dangerous to be out and exposed like that, but she said she needed the air. And could I argue? The house still smelled of death, and André smelled of sickness. It made the air inside the house heavy and depressing. Once, she used the shovel to kill a zombie that came wandering into the garden, but other than that, she wasn't bothered. Max was in the ground just before lunch, and Shadia built a cairn at the site with rocks found in neighboring flowerbeds.

She returned to the house and cleaned up. The water was still running, though we had no idea how. Could the water plant run without power? Or maybe it had a generator? I mean, we did have water if the power went out regularly, so maybe it just ran on its own? I had no idea; I wasn't an engineer. While the water wasn't warm, at least we could shower and wash things off, so she did just that. While she was still in the shower, André woke.

"Kit," he croaked, almost making me fall out of my chair, he scared me so much.

"Hey, dude," I answered, turning to look at him. "How're you feeling?"

"Like crap, you know?"

I nodded and felt his forehead. It was burning hot and clammy with sweat.

Shadia had left the first aid kit, the notebook and pen, and the polaroid camera on the writing desk in his room, so I picked up the set and started taking his temperature. While the thermometer read him, I checked my watch and added a log to the book. Shadia had told me to do it before she went outside. She was afraid for him, or of him, I wasn't sure which. Now that the fever was raging through his body, she didn't want to miss anything. As I flipped through the book, I saw that Shadia had taken notes on his health from the time she took over the record. These notes were much more informative than what was in the book when I had read it the first time.

The thermometer beeped, and I pulled it out of his mouth, reading the temperature before writing it in the book.

"It's bad, isn't it?" André asked, his voice hoarse.

"No," I lied and put the book down.

I helped him drink a little from the bottle of water on the nightstand.

"You're a bad liar, you know," he said when I lowered his head to the pillow again. His voice was a little clearer now.

"Too bad. Can I look at your shoulder?"

He made a face but moved. He was shirtless, his chest shining with the sweat, but the wound looked as it had the other times

I'd seen it. I took a photo of it anyway, just in case Shadia wanted it.

"Hey, Kit?" André asked.

"Yeah?" I answered, focusing on writing the time and date on the back of the picture.

"When are we eating?"

I stopped writing. "You hungry?"

He smacked his lips. "Yeah."

"Well, that's good. Having an appetite is good."

He looked away. "Yeah."

Shadia entered the room then, her hair still wet from the shower. She was dressed in clothes I'd never seen before. I didn't ask where they came from. She'd looted the closets for clean clothes for all of us yesterday. She was carrying a tray with three bowls of something, a plate with bread, and three cups.

"Oh, good, you're up," she said, putting the tray on the writing desk beside the notebook. "You hungry?"

"Starving," André answered, his eyes closed.

I handed Shadia the picture. She read what I'd written on the back, mouthing the temperature and tilting her head. I nodded and turned away. Forty degrees Celsius was high. Too high.

Shadia shook her head and tucked the picture into the notebook. Before she gave anything to André, we helped him into a sitting position. Then, she had him swallow two Paracet, hoping to bring his fever down.

The bowls contained vegetable noodle soup. André was barely able to get down a few spoons before he put the bowl down.

"You OK?" I asked.

He nodded and leaned back against the wall, closing his eyes and pressing his hands over his stomach. Shadia shook her head when I opened my mouth to ask if he was sure, and I returned my attention to my own soup, frowning. If this frustration, this helplessness was how Shadia felt with me, I had no idea how she'd stuck with me for this long. It made my respect for her grow, even as my worry for André stayed at the front of my mind.

The bread was hard and stale, but dipping it in the broth loosened it up and made it edible. The mugs contained juice. It was room temperature but still tasted of the fruity freshness of oranges.

By the time we were done with our meal, André was asleep again, and Shadia carefully wheeled me out of the room and into the one we shared before returning to help André.

"How was it?" I asked as she pulled the door to behind her.

"Still forty degrees," she said, shaking her head. "The Paracet didn't work."

"How can it not work?"

"I don't know."

She shook her head again and headed down the stairs, leaving me alone in the room. I considered going back to bed, knowing it would be the smart thing to do, but I wasn't feeling all that bad, surprisingly. Yesterday had been a mess of emotions and activity, but despite a somewhat short fuse on my temper and being more light and sound sensitive than usual, I was OK. Probably an adrenaline-high after yesterday. So instead of going to bed, I started looking around the house.

The room Shadia and I were using looked to have been a guest room for some time. There were no pictures on the dressers or nightstand, and only winter clothes and spare duvets in the closet. The attached bathroom was as good as empty of anything personal and only had some standard soap and towels. André's room had belonged to one of the two teenage boys. The walls were plastered with posters of girls in bikinis resting on the hoods of Ferraris. There was a football in one corner and a row of books standing on a shelf above the writing desk. They all seemed like books on health, and I hadn't given them much attention. So what was in the rest of the rooms? And where was the smell of death coming from?

I'd noticed the scent the day before when we first entered the house, but I'd been too emotionally used up to give it much thought. When I came out of the shower yesterday, I was too tired to consider it, and I fell asleep the moment Shadia tucked me into the bed. The scent was still there when I woke today, but weaker. Now, awake and curious, I wanted to know where it came from.

I opened the door beside the one leading to André's room, and my first thought was that the walls were painted black, but they were actually covered in posters. Some of bands and mythical creatures, some of tarot decks and movies. They'd been hung above one another, from floor to ceiling, hiding whatever color the walls had originally been. The bed was made with red covers, and the desk was almost hidden under the many papers that littered it.

Rolling closer, I lifted some of the papers. They were drawings. The artist had drawn the same group of creatures again and again. A hairy dwarf with a battle-ax, a hafling dressed in a hat, an elf with a bow, and a tiefling in full armor with sword and shield. It had been some time since I last played Dungeons and Dragons, but this looked like an adventuring party if I'd ever seen one, even if a Paladin tiefling was uncommon. I liked it.

I looked through a few more of the drawings, seeing scenes from what I guessed were the party's adventures.

The next door was at the end of the hall, and as I rolled closer, the smell of death grew stronger. It wasn't by much, but enough that I was prepared for what I might see in there when I opened the door.

Someone, my guess was Shadia, had opened the window before they closed the door yesterday, letting the smell out, trying to hide it. But she couldn't hide what lay on the bed.

It was a mess of blood, bone, and maggots. There was dried blood almost everywhere, dragged around by dog paws. The bodies were mostly whole, but one of the legs had been gnawed off and pulled to the other side of the room, where Max must have eaten it.

I stared at that gnawed on bone, not sure what to feel. Horrified, I was sure. Instead, I was empty and cold. Too shocked to feel properly.

The rest of the bodies were liquifying and writhing with bugs and maggots. Something had oozed through the sheets and into a pool on the floor.

I distantly wondered where the two kids were, for these were clearly the adults.

The stairs creaked, and I spun around. Shadia stood at the top of the stairs, resting one hand on the banister and looking at me.

"He ate them, didn't he?" I asked, feeling something move in my throat.

Shadia nodded and came toward me. "He had no choice, *habibi.* He was starving. He did what he had to do to stay alive."

"That's why he turned." I swallowed. "If he'd only eaten his food, I'm sure he would have been fine. Why couldn't he just eat his regular food? It contains processed meat, doesn't it? He wouldn't have turned then, he ..."

Shadia reached me and bent, wrapping her arms around me. "His food was in a cupboard with a lock on; there was no way he could get to it."

I hiccupped and swallowed a sob. "It's not fair."

"No, it's not."

All the feelings that had been buried under shock started flowing back, and I cried into Shadia's shoulder, holding her as close as I could. If I let her go, I might drown in my own tears. Tears for Max and what he had to do to survive, and still he died. Tears for the world that had changed around us. Tears for my friends and family that were taken by the parasite; who died and turned and would eat me if they got the chance. Tears for us left alive in this world of the dead.

20

A scream cut through my sleep, and I tumbled out of bed and onto the floor before I'd even opened my eyes. The screaming stopped and was replaced by mumbling.

Looking around, I noticed that the open window showed a grey sky, and the air was fresh and cool.

"Shadia?" I asked, lifting myself into my wheelchair. She wasn't on her side of the bed, so she must be on guard somewhere in the house. Was she the one screaming? No. Even in my sleep-groggy state, I would have recognized her voice. Wouldn't I?

"Here," Shadia answered from somewhere outside our room, and I breathed a sigh of relief.

"What's going on?"

I rolled into André's room but stopped in the doorway.

Shadia was sitting on the bed beside André, who was staring at her with big eyes and trying to push her away. He was too weak to be any threat, and Shadia held his arms to his chest trying to calm him down. André's eyes jumped to me as I came through the door, and he tried to pull away from Shadia.

"It's OK," she said, using the voice she used when one of her pupils got hurt. "It's just Kit, remember?" André looked at

127

Shadia, then at me, then at her again. "And I'm Shadia. You saved us, right?"

He stopped mumbling and stared at her for a long moment. "On a truck," he finally breathed.

"Yes. You helped us onto the roof and brought us to your safe house."

André nodded before his eyes started jumping around the room. "Where are we?"

"You don't remember?" I asked, rolling a little closer. He shook his head. "What's the last thing you remember?"

He bit his lower lip and thought for a moment. Even in the dim light from the moon, I could see his eyes were glazed with fever. It looked like he was asleep when he wasn't focusing on anything. "I was ... taking care ... of my subjects. Didn't want to leave them to suffer after I left, you know."

"The day before we left," Shadia said, glancing at me before carefully letting André's hands go. They stayed on his chest.

"Where are we?" he asked again.

"In a house. You got a fever, so we've stayed here for two days now," Shadia answered, dragging her hands across her face to hide a yawn.

"Oh."

"How are you feeling?" I asked when Shadia only looked at him.

André yawned before he answered. "Tired. Hungry. Warm."

As if for the first time noticing that he was mostly naked, and lying under a sheet that was clinging to his sweaty body, he blushed.

"I'll get you some food," Shadia said. "If I can take your temp again, and you'll take another Paracet."

André nodded reluctantly.

128

I rolled back so I wouldn't be in the way as Shadia found the thermometer and started writing things down in the logbook. When she was done, she watched as André swallowed two Paracet with half a mug of water, before she found another sheet and exchanged it for the clammy one.

As soon as she left, André waved for me to come closer. "Why are we here?" he whispered.

I blinked at him. "Didn't you listen just now?"

"Listen to what?"

"Shadia just told you that you got sick, so we're waiting here for you to get better."

"Oh." His eyes became even more glassy if that was possible. "Who's Shadia?"

"The woman who just left?"

"Oh," he said again, but his eyes were as confused as they had been when he asked.

"André, what's my name?"

He looked at me for a long time before he started looking around the room as if looking for clues.

Before he could answer, Shadia returned. She was carrying a plate filled with apple pieces. She sat on the edge of the bed and held out a piece. André stared at it for a long moment before he gingerly bit into it. The crunch of the apple made him wince, but he chewed and swallowed. For a long moment, he sat still, the skin around his lips growing pale, before he took the rest of the piece in his mouth.

André ate three applepieces, his face getting paler and his chewing harder with each piece. When Shadia tried to persuade him to eat another piece, he looked like he was going to throw up, and she pulled back.

She sighed and glanced at me before standing and walking

downstairs again. André and I sat in silence, him with his eyes closed and breathing heavily, me watching him, unsure what to do or say.

When Shadia returned, she carried another plate, this one with what looked like cut-up bierwurst. She placed it on the nightstand and sat on the edge of the bed. André scooted as far against the wall as he could get, but didn't argue as she fed him a piece at a time. Rather the opposite. It looked like she couldn't move fast enough or be close enough as he almost grabbed for her hand each time it came near with a piece. His eyes were still as glassy as ever.

I shuddered. "I'm going back to the bedroom."

"I'll join you when I'm done here," Shadia answered, not taking her eyes off André. I wasn't sure if she was concerned or afraid. I knew I was afraid.

"I can stay if you want."

Finally, she looked at me. "No, it's OK. Get some rest, *habibi*."

"If you say so."

I waited for another few heartbeats before I backed out of the door and rolled back to our room. I was too awake to go back to sleep, so I rolled to the window and looked out onto the street. It was empty and quiet, bathed in the light of the stars and a half-moon.

Shadia came into the room almost half an hour later. She slumped down on the bed, stifling another yawn. I rolled closer to her.

"How is he?" I asked.

"Asleep now, thankfully, but his fever isn't going down. I think it's going up, and the pills don't work." She shook her head. "I tried to ask him a little about how we got here, but he didn't remember anything. Every now and again, he'd ask me the same questions again and again."

"He doesn't know us either," I said. "He asked who you were after you left, and he didn't know my name when I asked." Shadia cursed and buried her face in her hands. "So what do we do?"

"I don't know. I honestly don't know. If it is the bite, there is no cure. But what if it isn't? What if it's an allergic reaction or something? I don't know. I'm a kindergarten teacher, not a doctor." Her voice was rising in volume as her eyes grew wider and wider.

"Hey, it's OK," I said, grabbing her hands and making her focus on me. "No one's blaming you for this, you hear?" She looked away, so I squeezed until she winced and turned back to me. "No one is blaming you, so you have to stop blaming yourself, OK?"

"That's easier said than done."

"I know, but try?"

She sighed. "Fine, I'll try."

"Thank you." I lifted her hands and kissed them. "And I think the best thing you can do right now is sleep."

"I can't. Someone has to stand guard."

"I'll do that. Or, you know, sit guard." I smiled at the bad joke, trying to lighten the mood. Shadia didn't smile, but there was a small twinkle in her eye. "I'm really awake anyway."

"Just promise to wake me if you get tired, OK? It's important that you get as much rest as you can."

I didn't agree with her but knew her too well to argue. Instead, I made my way into the bed with her and pulled the duvet aside. When she curled under it, I tucked her in and lay spooning her until her breathing became deep and her body twitched in sleep.

One of the things that annoy me the most about being in a wheelchair is how much noise it makes. I'd always been a night owl, sitting awake long into the night to game or read or draw, so I learned how to move my body without making much noise at all. Now, though, I didn't have that luxury. The chair made its noises, and there was nothing I could do about it. So, as I rolled my way from room to room on the second floor and looked out the windows to make sure no zombies were drawn to us or anything else came our way, I couldn't help but feel I was waking Shadia and André with every move. There was the ticking of the wheels, my hands against the steel push-bar, even the rubber against the floor. The creaking of the straps keeping my feet in place, and the small bumps I made as I knocked into something with my feet or back as I tried to move through the unfamiliar terrain. Not to mention my own breathing and muffled curses at all of these sounds. But it didn't seem to affect the sleepers at all, so after a while, I stopped with my mumbling and did my rounds in relative silence.

The sun was rising by the time I started to yawn, but I was set on taking just one more round before waking Shadia.

When I got to our room, movement through the window caught my attention. Backing up, I looked down at the road.

A car was making its way down the street at a crawl. I could see the outline of the people in the front seats, but no details.

My eyes jumped to look for the bodies we'd left behind the first day, but Shadia had pulled them all into the garage, out of sight from the road. But what if the people in the car noticed the blood on the pavement? What if they came to investigate? As anxiety built in my chest, I tried to tell myself there was no reason they would investigate the blood. There had been blood on the streets back in town; we'd even seen some blood on the street here and there as we walked from the car, so why should this dried pool be any different? Just someone unlucky who met their end, no reason to come closer or to try and solve the mystery of who the blood had belonged to.

The car reached the driveway and was almost past when it stopped.

No. Why would it stop?

The car backed up until the driver could look directly into the driveway. It stood there for a long time before the back door on the driver's side opened, and a man stepped out. It took my panicked brain a second to recognize Nicholas. He was leaning on a cane but seemed otherwise in good health. Shame.

He hobbled into the driveway, looking at the blood on the asphalt and then lifting his eyes to look at the house.

No, not the house, I realized, but the broken door. Stupid, stupid, stupid! Why hadn't we thought about fixing it? Or finding somewhere else to hide?

I wanted to wake Shadia, wanted to warn her, prepare her, something, but was afraid that my movement would catch his attention. So instead, I sat and watched as Nicholas stood in the driveway and took in the house, his eyes shining in the growing light.

A voice carried to me as someone inside the car leaned out the open door. I didn't dare take my eyes of Nicholas but could bet it was another man. Nicholas answered what must have been a question. He took one last look at the door before turning and made his way back to the car.

The driver's door opened, and the man there moved to step out, but Nicholas waved him back inside before crawling in himself. In the fiery light of the rising sun, I saw the pain on his face as he pulled the leg I'd bitten into the car before closing the door.

The car stood silent for a few seconds before it started its crawl up the street again.

I let out a deep breath and slumped back in my chair. I could feel my heart beating against my ribcage, wanting to break free, and my breathing came in heavy gulps. That had been too close.

"What was that?"

The voice made me shriek, and I clapped a hand over my mouth to muffle it. The car was out of sight and earshot, but I still feared them hearing me. Turning, I looked at Shadia. She was sitting up in the bed, eyes on me.

Taking a few calming breaths, I rolled over and told her what I'd seen. She stayed still the entire time, not asking questions or interrupting. Not even when I started having trouble finding the right words as the adrenalin finally started leaving my body.

"Well, we can't leave," she said when it was clear I was done. "Not with André the way he is."

"But we can't stay either," I argued. "What if they come back to … to …" I rolled my fingers in irritation before the word came to me. "Investigate the broken door?"

Shadia pulled a hand through her hair. "I don't think we have much choice right now."

I opened my mouth to speak, but she shook her head. When I closed my mouth, she reached out and pulled at me. I made my way from the chair onto the bed, and she wrapped me in the duvet and spooned me this time.

"You just sleep now, OK, and I'll think of something. I always do," she whispered against my hair.

"You shouldn't have to think of something all the time," I said, unable to keep my eyes open but feeling like crap for letting them slide shut.

She kissed me behind the ear. "Sleep on it for me."

I tried, but couldn't stay asleep even if I wanted to. The rest of the day went by in a daze. André kept falling in and out of consciousness, his memories more and more fragmented every time he woke up. I was exhausted and in pain as well, feeling sick and hating it because I knew it was my own fault for moving around so much during the night.

The car came back down the road around dinner time, driving a lot faster without slowing as it passed our driveway. I couldn't help feeling like they knew we were here. Like they were playing with us. But what could we do about it? A big, fat load of nothing. It made me grumpy, and I snapped at André the one time I helped feed him. I also snapped at Shadia almost every time I saw her. Finally, she had enough.

"OK, that's it," she said as I told her how sucky everything was for maybe the hundredth time that day, making sure to mention how useless we were. "I know you are tired and stressed, but so am I. I don't just have you to deal with anymore, but a dying man as well, you understand? I know your life sucks, and this ... the situation hasn't made it any better, but I am so over you biting my head off every time I try to lighten the mood. You hear me, Katerina Ingunn Tanum?"

The use of my full name shocked me out of my irritation, and I took a deep, calming breath. "I'm sorry," I said and leaned closer to kiss her. It was meant to be comforting, a wall for her to rest against, but the moment our lips met, her hands were in my hair, pulling me closer. There was desperation on her lips. Desperation to forget the boy lying across the hall; to forget the man hunting us, to forget the world. I didn't want to forget, but my body responded anyway.

Arching toward her, I let her arms wrap around me and take the weight off my body. She lifted me from the chair and drew me onto the bed and onto her. Her hand was knitted in my hair, pulling, just in that area between pain and pleasure. I moaned against her lips, my hand moving down her waist, resting on her hip, fingers slipping below the waistband of her pants, forgetting that she was on her period. Rolling to the side, we stared at each other for a long moment.

Something wet hit the floor across the hall, closely followed by the scent of stomach acid.

We broke apart so fast the pull at my hair made me yelp. Shadia mumbled a 'sorry', kissed the top of my head, and was out the door before I had even begun moving into my chair. Sometimes, I cursed the slowness of the contraption, almost forgetting how it also freed me from the confines of the bed.

Shadia was talking rapidly by the time I made it into André's room, stroking the vomiting man across the back and trying to comfort him. Tears were spilling down his face as bloody stomach acid fell from his lips to pool on the floor in a red mess.

"Holy crap," I mumbled, pulling the edge of my t-shirt across my nose and mouth, trying to keep out the stench. "What's going on?"

"What do you think?" Shadia snapped, not taking her eyes off André. The furrow in her brow told me she was snapping out of fear, not anger.

André fell back on the bed, moaning and clutching his stomach. His face was glowing with sweat, and his eyes were shut so tight one might forget he even had them. His lips were drawn back in a snarl of pain, blood coloring his teeth like pink lipstick.

"Is this what I think it is?" I asked, rolling to the edge of the pool on the floor.

Shadia shook her head, but it wasn't a denial. She was afraid and didn't want my guess to be right.

"What do we do?" I asked, my voice wavering.

"I don't know, OK? I don't know."

André let out a howl of pain that made my ears ring. Shadia jumped off the bed as the boy curled up, his bowels letting loose on their own. Almost before the smell, I saw the red seep through the sheet around him.

"Shadia," I said, grabbing her hand and pulling her away. "He's dying."

Shadia fell to her knees, not caring about the blood or the vomit, and started crying.

Excerpt from Medical Notebook

After the worm has moved to the brain, the body starts to fight it. The host starts craving meat, but instead of strengthening their own body, they feed the worm, which in turn lays eggs in the stomach. When the eggs hatch, the new worms start eating the host, leading to the bloody vomit and stool, and eventual death, as stomach acid spreads through the body and burns it up from the inside.

At the host's death, every worm except the ones nestled in the brain and stomach dies from starvation.

21

"You called this meeting, so what is it about?" Kenneth, my NAV counselor, asked.

"I'm worried that you do not fully believe Katerina's situation," Dr Mathias, my doctor, answered, leaning his folded hands on the table.

"Of course I'm taking her situation seriously, but there is only so much I can do," Kenneth answered, glancing at Shadia and me. We were sitting at the other end of the table, Shadia behind me.

"So what can we do?" I asked. "You said I would get disability support this time, that there was no way they couldn't give it to me." I motioned to my crutches before pushing my sunglasses higher on my nose. I was wearing them and a hat inside, the roof lamps too bright today. I hadn't really slept last night, too worried about this meeting. The tiredness could only work in my favor, though, couldn't it? Making me look half as sick as I felt.

Kenneth sighed. "I really believed it would go through this time."

"But it didn't," Shadia answered. "They used the fact that they don't know how sick she is against her."

"Now, I don't–" Kenneth began, but Shadia shook her head, and he closed his mouth.

Satisfied, Shadia found the notification letter and started reading out loud. *"... Decline your application for Disability Support. It is our opinion that you do not meet the qualifications needed for this support. You have not been through Work Clarification on the basis that you are too sick to keep to the program. But without the program to estimate your sickness percentage, we do not know if you are more than fifty precent disabled or not."* She put the letter onto the table and looked at Kenneth. *"It says right here that they can't give her disability support because she is too sick to figure out how sick she is."*

I put a hand over Shadia's to quiet her. "The point is that there is a way to fix this: I go through Work Clarification."

"I really do not think that is necessary," Kenneth said, leaning back in his chair. "We know how sick you are."

"But they don't," I said. "The caseworkers in Tønsberg don't know, and that's the point." I swallowed the sudden lump in my throat. "I don't think Work Clarification will be good for me. I'm afraid going through with it will use up what little energy I have left, but that must be better than this limbo I'm in right now. I can hardly leave my home because I'm too sick. I spend most days in bed, and I can't even walk from my bedroom to the bathroom without support. Sometimes I even need help getting up from the toilet."

"And that's why we won't go through with Work Clarification," Kenneth said as I drew a deep breath and hurriedly dried the tears that had escaped my eyes. "We complain about this decision, we fight it, but we won't make you sicker to do so."

"But they don't believe me." I hiccupped, angry at myself for crying and angry at the system for putting me in this position.

"Then we make them believe." Kenneth turned to Dr Mathias. "On your last evaluation, you wrote that you don't see Katerina getting better any time soon. Do you still believe that?"

Dr Mathias nodded. "Yes. Katerina has a severe case of M.E. If *she starts getting better, which I do not believe will happen any time soon if at all, it will be a long time before she can consider returning to work. Even if she woke up tomorrow and was completely healthy, there would be months, possibly years, of physical therapy before she could get back to a normal lifestyle."*

"Understood," Kenneth said. "So we complain, we ..."

My stomach turned. Heaving, I fell to the floor, skinning my knees on the stone steps, and fought not to throw up.

I blinked awake, for a moment thinking I was actually going to throw up before I realized the sounds weren't coming from me.

Groaning and moaning and heaving echoed down the hall.

Almost falling, I hurried out of bed and into my chair, not caring that I wasn't wearing any pants, and made my way into André's room. He was tossing and turning on the bed, bloody vomit dripping from his mouth as he choked. Where was Shadia?

Cursing, I hurried forward, the chair hitting against the bed and almost pinching my hand before I flipped the brakes and reached for André. Twice, he twisted out of my hands, his arms and legs dancing around. Finally, I got a grip and turned him over. Vomit oozed from his mouth and onto the pillow, and I gagged at the smell.

"Come on," I begged, stroking his shoulder. "Just get it out and breathe." I didn't dare think about the way his body twitched. It was minor now that I'd gotten him on his side and he wasn't drowning anymore, but it was still there. I could feel it ripple just under his skin.

The ooze of vomit stopped, and André started breathing a little easier again.

"There you go," I mumbled before I carefully eased him onto

his back.

The sound of footsteps on the stairs reached me, and I turned to see Shadia enter the room. She almost walked into my chair before she noticed us.

"What happened?" she asked.

"He started vomiting," I answered and scooted away from André, letting my arms rest.

Shadia's jaw tensed, but she didn't say anything, just moved my chair out of the way.

Together, we dragged and pushed until he lay with his back against the wall. If he started throwing up again, it would fall right out of his mouth instead of choking him.

When he was secure, Shadia started cleaning up. He'd soiled himself as well as vomited. I wanted to help, but Shadia asked me to rest, and I didn't complain. My arms were weak and numb after holding him on his side. He wasn't heavy, but I couldn't take much.

It took Shadia twenty minutes to get all the filthy clothes out of the room. It lessened the smell a little, but we still needed to clean his body to get it all away, and we didn't dare open the window, in case Nicholas or some of his men drove by and heard André mumbling or something. Chances were small that it would happen, but we didn't want to take the risk it. We didn't even use a flashlight as Shadia cleaned up, relying on the light of the moon.

When Shadia had all the supplies she needed to clean his body, I moved to leave. André wasn't twitching anymore. His arms and legs lay limp, but he was still in the grip of a fever, mumbling in his sleep and tossing his head weakly.

"You'll be OK?" I asked quietly.

Shadia only nodded, her jaw set but face otherwise empty.

"Sure you don't want my help?"

She turned and looked at me, forcing a smile. "You'll help me more by taking care of yourself, so I can focus on taking care of him."

I nodded and left, more than ready to get myself cleaned up. It felt like my whole skin was crawling with germs.

When I was done in the bathroom, I checked in on Shadia and André, but she was still cleaning him, a disgusted look on her face. In any other situation, that expression would have been funny, but it wasn't now. I left them in peace.

Exhausted, I pushed myself into our bedroom and crawled onto the bed.

It was as my eyes closed that I remembered the ending of my dream had been wrong. The meeting had dragged on and on, trying to make a plan that in the end didn't work.

NAV was a rollercoaster that had given me more anxiety and taken more energy than anything else in my life. They were supposed to be there to help the sick, but there were so many rules and loopholes that the patient didn't stand a chance. Luckily, I didn't fight alone. I had Shadia and my parents, but it was still a long fight we didn't know when we'd win.

Sleep was poor after that. I woke multiple times. Sometimes it was my own fault. I'd fallen asleep on top of the covers and woke when Shadia tried to move them over me. Another time, I was sure someone was trying to get into the house, but the sounds were gone the moment I woke up. It was André that woke me most of the time, mumbling and raving. Sometimes he would scream or groan so loud it made me jump almost out of bed before I was even awake. In the end, I gave up on sleep sometime before dawn.

I was preparing breakfast when André screamed again, followed by a hard thud. Dropping the can I'd been opening, I rolled toward his room so fast I almost missed the door and sailed down the stairs.

André was face-down on the floor, his body rigid and vibrating. Shadia was by his side, trying to turn him over.

Cursing and calling his name, I stopped beside them and slid out of the chair. Touching him, I felt the muscles under his skin. They were taut as a rope, every muscle in his body tightened as far as they could without breaking a bone. Even as I thought it, I heard a snap from his arm followed by a gurgling sound, like screaming under water.

"No, no, no, no," Shadia mumbled.

André's face was just as stiff as the rest of his body, lips drawn back, bared teeth pressed together so hard I heard them grind, and his eyelids were wide open, his eyes jumping around without seeing anything.

"André," I said, gripping his face with both hands and trying to get him to look at me. "André, come on." There was no reaction. I looked up at Shadia, but her eyes were empty.

"I don't know what to do," she said.

There was another snap, this time from André's chest.

My eyes flew back to his face. "Please, relax!" His eyes suddenly stilled on me, staring. I wasn't sure if he was seeing me or not, but I forced a smile to my face, just in case. "That's right. Look at me. I know it hurts, but you need to breathe. It's hard, I know, but try, OK?"

A tremor ran through him, starting in his chest and spilling outwards, like the ripples on a lake after someone threw a stone into it. His breathing was ragged and hard, barely there and shallow, like there wasn't room in his lungs for any air with the muscles so tight. Then he stopped. He just stopped breathing.

"No! Don't you dare! Don't. Please." My voice was barely a whisper.

His body slumped, his head resting heavily against my hands. His eyes were more empty than I'd ever seen them.

At his stillness, Shadia seemed to snap back to reality. She pushed me away and checked his pulse. I knew it wouldn't be there, but I was calmed by the action. It proved Shadia knew what she was doing. She rested her ear against his mouth, then pushed her hair away from her eyes as she sat up, starting CPR. His chest looked loose, somehow, like his ribs were too broken to offer up even a semblance of resistance.

I don't know how long we sat there, trying to get André to wake up, to live again. I started crying. I didn't know André that well, but he deserved better than this. Deserved better than to die in some unknown person's bed, two strange women by his side, the world outside teeming with zombies and men hunting us. He deserved better.

When Shadia gave up, we sat on the floor for a time, looking at the empty body before us.

"I'm going to prepare him for burial," Shadia said, her voice hoarse but in charge. "He deserves that." I nodded. "Can you write this down in the book?"

When I looked up at her, she nodded to the notebook that André had started and Shadia had taken over. I nodded again.

Shadia forced a smile and turned away.

Keeping my eyes on the notebook, I scribbled down what had happened while Shadia cleaned and dressed him again. André hadn't had anything left to soil himself with this time, but he had sweated through his clothes and the bedding.

I was about to leave the room, Shadia still not done, when a thought struck me. My bet was on the bite being the cause of his death, but there was no way for us to be sure, as he'd walked around with it for so long. But what if it was? And even if it wasn't, what if this parasite was like the virus in *The Walking Dead?* What if we all had it, and it takes us over when we die anyway?

OK, no, that didn't make sense, but what about the baby I saw? I'd forgotten to ask him about that, but I was too tired to curse my awful memory. My brain was jumping to conclusions because I was so tired. But even if he wouldn't, I didn't want to take any chances.

Rolling into the master bedroom, I found a set of ugly sheets and used a knife to tear it into strips.

I rolled back into the bedroom, where Shadia had just pulled a pair of jeans onto André's body. She looked up from her work when I rolled to the head of the bed and started tying one of the strips of fabric to the bed-leg.

"What are you doing?" she asked, voice low. As if afraid to wake him.

"I don't wanna risk him coming back to life while we sleep," I said, not looking at her.

She stiffened. "You think he will?"

"I don't know, but I'm not taking any chances."

I looked up at her, almost expecting her to stop me. Instead, she put out a hand, and I gave her one of the improvised ropes. She bound it around his left wrist and snuck the end down between the bed and the wall. She'd have to crawl under the bed to fasten it, but I didn't say anything, just returned to my own wrist. It was all floppy, the bones inside crushed by the seizure. I could feel the bones move when I touched him. It

146

almost made me start crying again, but I was able to keep the tears at bay as I moved to his legs, where I was able to secure both.

Shadia still wasn't quite done with her cleaning, so I left her to it, trusting she would let me know if something happened.

Car doors slammed, forcing me out of my slumber, and I turned to wake Shadia. The room was dark, the sunlight kept out by thick curtains, and I was alone. I'd cried myself to sleep and had apparently slept for hours. My face was dry and sore after the tears, but the fatigue in my body had lessened.

Voices drifted through the open window, and I froze. I knew I'd heard car doors, but for some reason, I blamed it on a dream. I hadn't really believed there was a car outside.

Hurrying as silently as I could, I made my way into my chair and rolled to the window. Moving up under the curtains, I tried to look out.

The sky was that pale blue of a just set sun. No stars or moon yet, but they were just around the corner. The light was weak enough that I didn't need sunglasses, which was good, for they lay on my bedside table, forgotten in my rush. Squinting, I turned my gaze to the road.

Two black cars stood there, idling. All the doors were open, and only the drivers were left in their seats. I couldn't see anyone else, but I could hear men talking.

"... they're here?" one of them said.

"No. Can't picture them hanging around, but they may have

left a clue as to where they were going," another answered.

"Why does he think they stopped here?" A third voice asked. Crap, how many were there?

"The door. The blood in the driveway. That strip of blood there. He said it looked like what a wheelchair might leave behind. It's clear someone passed through here not long ago, and it might as well be 'em, right?" The second voice again.

As if on cue, I heard something crash into the front door, and one of the men cursed. "They've blocked it from the inside," he said.

There was a lot more bumping and cursing before someone yelled for Nicholas.

Shadia appeared in the doorway, a rope of shredded fabric in her hands. I'd sunk down along the wall as they tried the door, not wanting the drivers to see me. Our eyes met at the name, and I stopped breathing for a second. What would he do with us if he found us?

Shadia waved for me to move, forming words with her lips that I couldn't understand. However, her movement shocked me out of my frozen state, and I started looking for our bags. They'd stood beside the door, but they weren't there now.

"I got them," Shadia whispered when I looked up at her. "Come on." She started down the hall as quietly as she could.

The voices still drifted through the window, but I couldn't hear any words. Taking a deep breath, I rolled into the hallway and opened the door to André's room.

André lay as we'd left him, but the sight of him sent a chill through me. It took me three more deep breaths before I was able to roll into the room and look through the window.

Two men were in the garden, standing at Max's grave. As I watched, Nicholas came limping into view, supporting himself on a cane. He stopped at the grave, listening to the other two men talk. I couldn't hear them through the closed window, and I didn't dare open it.

Below, someone banged at the kitchen door.

Shadia hissed my name, and I turned to see her standing in the doorway, bags flung all around her, and my sunglasses and hat in hand.

"Come on," she hissed.

"Where are we going?" I whispered back.

"Getting out of here."

"How?"

"I made a way while you slept."

"What? Why?"

She sighed and knelt before me. "I heard them drive by a few hours ago and figured we should have a way out in case they came back. We couldn't leave earlier, but now …" Her eyes jumped to André's still form before moving back to me.

"There's nothing holding us back anymore," I whispered.

She nodded.

The banging stopped, then came a thump of something hitting a wall.

"Please, just go," I whispered, praying to a god I didn't believe in. "Just leave us alone."

Shadia slapped the hat on my head. "Come on."

I nodded, throwing a final look at André before I let her pull me away from the window. The door closed behind us with a strange finality.

We were halfway down the hall when someone knocked at the front door.

We both stopped, and I heard Shadia give a quiet yelp. Turning, I saw she'd clapped one hand over her mouth to stifle it.

"I know you're in there," Nicholas called, his voice muffled but clear enough through the hole in the door. "We just want to talk."

Shadia started moving again. Nicholas had gone quiet, but I could still hear the deep timbre of men talking. Then they got quiet as well.

Shadia was moving so slow as if afraid moving any faster would show them where we were.

"This is your last chance," Nicholas yelled, his voice seeming to make the world around me vibrate. "If you don't come out in the next ten seconds, I'll light the house on fire."

What? He wasn't serious, was he?

"Ten ..."

Did he know what would happen if he started a fire right now? We hadn't had rain in weeks. Adrenalin slammed into my system, making my fingers and lips tingle.

"Nine ..."

The fire would spread out of control, too fast for even him to be completely safe, and it wasn't like there were any firemen to put it out anymore.

"Eight ..."

Even he couldn't be that stupid, right? That desperate? I turned and looked up at Shadia. Her eyes were huge and afraid.

"Seven ..."

As if thinking the same thing, she turned us around and rolled me to our own bedroom. We had to see if he ment it or not.

"Six ..."

Moving under the curtains again, I looked out the window.

"Five ..."

Nicholas was standing in the middle of the driveway, leaning against his cane. The men were standing around him. It was too dark to see any details, but it looked like three of them were holding bottles.

"Four …"

"Are you sure this is a good idea?" one of the men asked in a low voice, barely audible.

"It is our mission to repopulate the earth, and we need every human on our side to do it," Nicholas answered. "Three …"

"But not like this," the other man continued, gesticulating. "Not by risking a fire that could level Oslo."

Without warning, Nicholas lifted his cane and swung it at the man. He didn't even have time to duck as it cracked against his shoulder.

"Two…" Nicholas lowered the cane as the other man lay on the ground, groaning. "Anyone else have any objections?" The other men shook their heads. "Good. One." Nicholas returned his attention to the house. "We gave you ample warning. Your time is up."

For half a second, nothing happened, and I hoped the other men in the group would be reasonable. They would understand the magnitude of what they were about to do. The hope died when fire flickered in their hand. In the light, I saw fabric stuffed down the top of bottles. The fools had made Molotov-cocktails.

"Now!" Nicholas ordered, and the men moved forward, out of my sight.

We could do nothing but listen as windows broke downstairs, followed by the smash of bottles breaking on the floor. The smell of alcohol swam up the stairs, closely followed by the sounds of fire, grabbing hold of fabric and wood.

Crap. They were really burning the house down. And we were stuck on the second floor.

23

Before I even had time to finish the panicked thought of being stuck, Shadia pulled me into the hallway again. The smell of smoke was already heavy in the air, but it hadn't begun to go hazy yet. We still had time.

As we moved, Shadia slung a bag into my lap, and I recognized it as my messenger bag. I secured it over my shoulder as Shadia handed me my sunglasses and stopped in front of the master bedroom, flinging open the door.

The master bedroom, the room where Max had eaten his owners after they died, spreading their bodies all over the place, was at the side of the house, so there were windows on all three walls. Those on the right looked over the garden, those on the left onto the street. The wall straight ahead was mostly one big closet, but there were small windows on both sides, looking into the neighboring garden. One of the windows was open, and the rest of our bags lay on the windowsill, waiting for us.

Shadia made her way to one of the smaller windows.

"What are we doing?" I asked as I followed.

She flung the rope she was carrying out the window and moved to secure the end to the bed. "Getting out," she answered. "There's a passage down there."

I rolled to the window and leaned out, looking into a small opening between the house and the fence. It was empty, but that didn't mean they weren't keeping an eye on it. Even if they hadn't noticed the passage, they would probably be in both the back yard at the front of the house. We could get out, but then what?

"OK, and where do we go from there?" I asked, turning back to see Shadia checking the knot would hold.

She froze, eyes going distant for a moment, then she shook her head. "We'll cross that bridge when we get there."

I considered answering with something snarky but had to clap my hand over my mouth to keep from coughing. OK, time to go.

Shadia stood. "You first."

"No, you go," I answered.

She opened her mouth, and something exploded downstairs. My chair jumped under me, and I screamed in shock. Shadia yelled my name and reached for me. Outside, someone yelled something. They must have heard me. Great.

My hands shaking with adrenaline and fear, I pushed to my feet. My legs started wobbling the moment I stood, pain lancing through them like lightning, but I didn't care, didn't give myself time to feel it. Instead, I climbed onto the windowsill and turned my back to the open sky. I'd never rappelled before and wasn't sure my legs could even support me bouncing off the wall, but there was no time like the present to try something new, right?

Grabbing the sheet-rope, I pushed my way out of the window.

My legs gave out the moment I tried bouncing off the wall, and I slapped into it instead, face scraping against the melting paint. The heat of the fire inside the house had penetrated the walls, and I could feel it trying to burn my cheek. I didn't let it. Somehow, I got my knees against the wall and supported my feet on one of the many knots of the rope. Gripping above the next knot, I moved my feet down to the next, and so on.

Shadia climbed out above me, heavy with bags but still able to climb much steadier than me.

I was two knots above the ground when something else inside the house exploded. This time, I managed not to scream as the window above me shattered and rained warm glass over us. The rope jerk in my hands before breaking. I fell to the ground and thudded against it, the air knocked from my lungs. But even as I gasped for breath, I tried to call for Shadia, afraid the fall would be too long for her.

She landed beside me and rolled, somehow able to keep her momentum. It wasn't a graceful landing, however, as all the bags pulled her balance in every directions. She wasn't hurt, however, and I allowed myself two seconds to breathe in relief. Or try to, at least.

I looked up at the window we'd just escaped through. The fire was licking at the walls around it, reaching out against the darkening sky.

The house had gone up quicker than I thought. It could hardly be more than a minute since they'd thrown the bottles. But we hadn't had rain in forever, and the house had been old and filled with fabric and flammables.

Shadia appeared and helped me sit up, looking me over for damage. I did the same with her. Satisfied, I threw one last look at the boiling walls, and another window shattered somewhere. I sent up a silent apology for André. No one would know he was dead. No one but us. This fire was his funeral pyre.

I sat there watching until my back stopped hurting. It didn't take long. I was full of adrenaline, but my lungs wouldn't stop complaining. They were dry and sore from the smoke and heat, which was still roiling around me. If I didn't move soon, I couldn't help but cough, and then Nicholas and his men would find us.

Turning, I made it onto all fours. Grabbing for my hat, I looked around. "Where to?" I whispered.

Shadia was looking around as well, chewing on her bottom lip. The smoke of the fire lay like a blanket around us, even this low. There was no wind to take it away.

"I can hardly see the end of the passage on both sides, so the men there shouldn't be able to see us, I think," Shadia said, glancing at me. "We can follow the fence and get to the road, maybe steal a car?"

"They left the doors open," I said, catching on. "Maybe they're arrogant enough to leave the keys in as well?"

Shadia snorted. "No doubt."

"The drivers stayed in the cars, though."

"I don't think they would have stayed there when the fireworks started."

I sighed, trying for nonchalance to hide my fear and worry.

In front of the house, someone said something. It wasn't a yell, so we couldn't make out the words, but I recognized the bass of male voices.

"Let's go," Shadia said and crawled past me.

Crawling along on all fours, Shadia in front and me behind, we stayed close to the fence and let the smoke hide us. It had grown even thicker in the short time we'd stopped, and I was glad for it, even if my throat hurt and my lungs desperately wanted me to cough. My eyes were burning, and tears were constantly trying to fix the burn, making me blink all the time.

Above, another window shattered, and fire leaped toward the sky. I reached for Shadia, wanting to protect her. At the same time, she flung herself around to grab at me. We buried our faces against each other as glass shards bounced off our heads and shoulders. When it stopped, we pulled back and looked at one another. I had to fight not to giggle hysterically, and Shadia must have seen it in my eyes, for she touched her lips to mine and whispered a shush, but I could see strange amusement in her eyes as well.

When my laughter was under control, we crawled on, and after what felt like forever, we reached the end of the passage.

The voices were clearer now, and I picked up a few words. Looking around the corner, I saw the shape of men moving in the smoke, but nothing distinct. No details. I couldn't even tell if one of them had a cane or not.

"... heard something," one of the voices said.

"But no one's come out. Maybe it was just something exploding?" another voice answered.

"No, that was a scream. I've heard enough of those lately to recognize it."

"You don't think they stayed inside and burned rather than be with us, do you?"

"Nah. No one's that stupid."

"Or smart."

"Hey! What did you say?"

I let them argue and moved closer to the fence again, looking at Shadia. Her eyes jumped to the shadow of the cars, and I nodded.

The fence scraping against our shoulders, we crawled on.

If the men could see this far, maybe they would think our shadows were just part of the fence.

To my left, the men were arguing openly now, having drawn another into their discussion. I both thanked and cursed them. Their argument would mask any noise we made, but it might also draw the rest of them to a position where they could see us.

The ground beneath me changed from tired grass to dirt. Breathing shallowly, I continued, forcing myself to stay calm despite my racing heart and hurting muscle. Focusing on Shadia's ass in front of me, I tried to not look at the men and not move too fast.

Nicholas's voice sounded above the others, making them fall silent. I stopped, afraid that my movement would catch their attention, despite the crackling of the huge fire.

"What is this?" Nicholas asked, his voice harsh.

"He said he thinks the girls are smart to stay away from us," one of the original voices said.

"I did not," the other original voice answered. "I just said that we should let them be. What right do we have to decide their future for them?"

I didn't dare turn to look at them, so I stayed frozen, listening.

Nicholas tsked. "But my dear brother, don't you know our sacred duty?"

"To repopulate the earth," the offender said, voice empty.

"Yes. And is it not then our duty to keep every mother safe? Even from themselves?"

"Yes." Still empty.

A small hope had flared inside me and died in the same instant. This guy didn't believe the nonsense Nicholas was saying, but he wouldn't help me either. He wasn't ready to break away, or maybe he was too afraid. He was no help to me.

Something crashed behind us, and I jumped. Glancing over my shoulder, I saw the roof of the house had collapsed, the fire reaching for the sky. It illuminated what had previously been hidden by smoke, and I could see small details in the shapes of the men now. The color of their clothes, the way they were turned toward the fire, watching.

This was our chance. If we lingered, they would see us just as clear as we now saw them. This was it.

I turned and met Shadia's eyes. She nodded and swung forward, rushing toward the nearest car. I followed, scraping my knees and fingers against stones and asphalt. My palms were protected by the gloves, making some sound but nothing loud enough to catch their attention with the raging fire so close, I hoped.

The fence disappeared from my side, and I almost toppled onto the sidewalk. Luck was the only reason I stayed up.

I glanced back, seeing the men even clearer now. They were turned away from us, thankfully. I faced forward, seeing Shadia scramble into the driver's seat of one of the cars. I rushed after her and pulled myself through the open back door, and sent a hurried thanks to whoever might be listening as I grabbed the door, swinging it shut. As I lunged across the backseat to close the other one, Shadia started the car with a roar.

Someone yelled as the doors slammed. I didn't look, didn't think, but tugged the other door closed and moved to climb into the front.

The car rushed forward and flung me into the backseat

again.

"You OK?" Shadia called.

I didn't answer, just pulled myself into the front seat and grabbed the door that had almost closed on its own.

Glancing in the rearview mirror, I saw nothing but smoke and the orange gleam of the fire. Without signaling, Shadia swung onto a side road. I was praying the men wouldn't catch up before we were out of sight.

We were in the open for what felt like forever, but finally, the road turned, and I breathed a small sigh of relief. The smoke had lessened, and I didn't doubt the men would have noticed the car if they looked in the right direction. We'd been lucky so far.

Something moved out of the smoke before us and slammed into the front of the car.

24

The car crunched against concrete, and I flew forward. Just before I struck the dashboard, the airbag let out and pushed me back against the seat as the car flipped over the wall and landed on its roof. Shadia's scream made my ears ring. If not for the airbag, I would have thumped my head against the roof, maybe broken my neck. As it was, I was stuck for half a heartbeat before the bag started deflating.

Somehow, I got my arms under me, and the landing on the roof was soft. I slipped from the bag's grasp and lay panting. Broken glass from the windows was everywhere, digging into my skin. They didn't cut, but it was uncomfortable.

"Shadia?" I turned to look for her and saw her legs as she crawled out through the broken window.

I was about to call for her again when her face appeared in the window. "Kit? Are you OK?" Blood was leaking from a wound in her forehead, coating most of her face.

"I could ask you the same thing," I answered.

Shadia touched her cut and winced, but she didn't take her eyes off me. "Come on; we got to go. Nicholas and his men must have heard the crash."

I undid my belt, turned onto all fours, and started crawling out of the shattered window. The moment I was out, Shadia reached for me, but I swatted her hands away and grabbed her face.

"Does your head hurt? Can you see me OK?" I asked, staring into her eyes. Her pupils looked normal, and she was furrowing her brow in irritation.

She pushed me away. "It's just a surface wound. They bleeds."

I grumbled again as she looked me over. All her movements seemed steady, and despite the bleeding, there didn't seem to be any swelling.

When she was happy with my own condition, she started rearranging her bags. As she worked, I looked myself over as well.

I was dressed in loose-fitting clothes, and both pants and t-shirt were shredded by the glass. I was bleeding from multiple cut, but not as bad as Shadia's. She had other small wounds as well, but nothing seemed serious on either of us. Nothing was broken, at least.

Panic moved in my stomach when I considered all the ways we could get infected now. Zombie blood in our open wounds would be enough. It wouldn't have to be more than a drop. I squeezed the panic by reminding myself that we had been staying away from meat for a reason. Even if we got zombie-eggs in us, they wouldn't survive without meat.

Shadia fished out an anti-bacterial spray and hurriedly sprayed it over most of her wounds, then over mine. She gave the bottle to me so I could spray her head, then she had me tie a t-shirt around her head to stop the bleeding. It all took barely two minutes.

Taking the bottle from me, she handed me a rucksack. I swung it onto my back as she grabbed her own rucksack and swung it around to carry it over her stomach. I noticed that my hat and one of the axes were gone, but I knew we'd dallied too long. It was a wonder Nicholas and his men hadn't found us already. At least I still had my glasses.

"Up you go," Shadia said, and I crawled onto her back.

Groaning, she stood up.

"You sure this is OK?" I asked. I was battered and bruised, and she had to be feeling the same.

"It's fine," she said and took a few steps away from the car. "It's only temporary anyway."

I didn't ask what she meant by that. We both knew we wouldn't get far with her carrying me, and we had to find an alternative. But first, we needed to get out of here.

Looking up, I saw the orange flicker of the fire in the haze. We weren't far away, just downhill of the house. As I watched the fire flicker and grow bigger, Shadia jogged down the street. Blood dripped from her chin and onto the ground, but by the time we reached the end of the street, most of what could drip away had already done so, and the trail we left behind was growing harder to follow.

Shadia stopped and turned, taking in the trail and shaking her head to get rid of a few more drops before she turned and started running across a lawn to our left. The uneven ground made me jostle up and down on her back, my grip almost slipping multiple times. It hurt, and I could only imagine it did the same for Shadia.

She continued without complaints, heading back the way we had come, but making sure to keep multiple houses and fences between us and the road.

At one point, we heard male voices again. They must have found the crash and would be following our trail soon.

Hopefully, Shadia's plan worked, and they would search in the wrong direction.

I would have expected my adrenaline to dissipate, but the strain of holding on to Shadia kept it pumping, making me jittery and restless. I stayed as still as I could and trusted in my wife. She knew what she was doing.

After about five more minutes of steady jogging, Shadia was panting and stumbling.

"You need to rest," I said in a low voice, but she shook her head. I squeezed with my legs, and she winced, her left leg almost giving out. "Yes. Now, get behind those bushes up ahead, and we can take a break."

I was afraid she would run right past them, but at the last moment, she turned into the driveway and walked alongside the tall bushes. At the other end of the garden, well hidden from the road, was a trampoline, and she stopped beside it and let me lower myself to the ground. The bushes were low and thin, but the trampoline hadn't been visible from the road, so we should be safe for now. Shadia crawled beneath it, and I followed.

Untangling the bags and rucksack, I pulled them off Shadia before I found drink, food, and pain killers. Handing one bottle to Shadia, I drank some of the water and took a pill before I ate one of the small bags of nuts and fruits we'd brought. It sat heavy in my stomach, but at least I wasn't getting sick and throwing it up. I could deal with heavy.

I sat there, staring at the grey world, trying to breathe deeply, and wasn't sure I could move. Everything was heavy now that I had time to relax. I could hardly even lift my arms to find my bandana in my messenger bag and drench it with water. When I held it over my mouth and nose, it made it a little easier to breathe in the smoky air, but not much.

I looked across my wounds, covering the visible ones with band-aids to keep them safe.

Beside me, Shadia's breathing was shallow and raspy, and I lay my wet bandana over her mouth and nose. She jumped at the touch, then took her first deep breath since we climbed out the window. I found her bandana and drenched it before tying it around my own face, then I looked over all her wounds, cleaning them and putting on band-aids. The head wound was still bleeding a little, so I left the t-shirt for now. It was already blood-soaked, so no use ruining another bandage.

I don't know how long we stayed there, or if we fell asleep or into a kind of waking coma, but the scent of rotting flesh was what woke me again. It had come creeping, hardly noticeable at first, until it felt like it wrapped around me, getting ready to smother me.

My heart beating too fast in my chest, I grabbed Shadia's hand. It twitched, and she sat up, poking her head against the underside of the trampoline before crouching. Grimacing, she grabbed the bandana that had fallen off her face and held it over her mouth and nose, looking around. Moving until I sat on my knees, I looked around as well.

The source of the smell had to be close, as there was still no wind, but at first, I couldn't hear anything. Then, finally, came the shuffling of feet on gravel. Leaning on one hand, I looked toward the thin hedge at our side.

A shape was shambling its way up the path.

Soundlessly, Shadia reached for my ax. It was strapped to her rucksack, the head wrapped in fabric so it wouldn't hurt us by accident. She moved as fast as she could to have it ready.

I crawled to the edge of the trampoline and watched the

shape as it moved. Any moment now, it would turn toward us.

Shadia came to my side and handed me her knife. I took it, not looking at her. The zombie didn't even seem to notice us as it walked along the fence on the other side of the hedge. It strained to get through, but couldn't, so it just shambled onward until it was out of view again, clothes and flesh tearing on the sharp branches.

After a glance at Shadia, I crawled to the other side of the trampoline. Shadia hissed my name, but I didn't stop before I could see the road. I waited, feeling Shadia's eyes on me. The zombie shambled on, making straight for the orange glow of the fire.

Blinking, I sat back on my haunches and looked at the fire. It must be so big that we didn't make a blip on the zombie's radar. The fact registered in the back of my brain, but I was too elated at the thought of us being momentarily invisible to the zombies to consider what it meant. We could use that.

I crawled back and told Shadia what I'd seen and surmised from it. She didn't argue but instead started wrapping up the ax again.

"We should get going," she mumbled, her eyes jumping around now that she was awake.

I wanted to argue, wanted to tell her we should stay here a little longer, but I knew she was right. Fighting while carrying me would be near impossible, so we should use the distraction of the fire as much as possible. But I did force her to slow down enough for me to check her head wound again. It had stopped bleeding, so I tossed the soaked t-shirt to where I'd left my own ruined clothes and cleaned the area off dried blood. I put band-aids over the scabbed-over wound and finally allowed her to leave the safety of the trampoline.

25

We spent the night in a two-story building that had been the home of a family of five. We stayed in the master bedroom, sleeping in shifts, and eating sparingly. The house only had potato chips–so many bags of potato chips–and baby food, so we ate the chips and were happy with that.

Sometime around midnight, my adrenaline-rush stopped. My body was plunged into a seizure so fast I didn't even have time to wake Shadia. She woke when I fell out of my chair by the window from shaking so hard. When she tried to help, my arm smacked her in the face. After a lot of back and forth, she was able to get me onto the bed, and to take a double dose of pain pills. I slipped into a restless sleep filled with nightmares, and woke with dancing limbs, but at least I slept.

The next morning, we debated whether to stay in the house or not. Shadia wanted to give me time to rest and recuperate after the events of the day before. I argued that it would make it easier for Nicholas to find us. We left around lunchtime, after I had gotten a few more hours of drug induced sleep.

The air smelled of smoke, and if we turned to look back, we could see the yellow light of fire against the sky, as well as smoke billowing above it. It seemed the fire had spread over night. Again, we had to take multiple breaks so Shadia wouldn't exhaust herself, and we ate and drank a little at each of those breaks. We didn't have enough food to be completely satiated, but the constant snacking kept the worst of the hunger at bay.

Around dinner time, we reached the top of the hill we'd been climbing for hours now. The houses had fallen away a few meters behind, but the top of the hill was dominated by a retirement home.

Shadia made a humming sound before walking around the corner of the E-shaped building and stopped in front of a bench by the doors.

"What're you doing?" I asked as I crawled from her back.

"I just need to take a quick look inside."

"Why?"

She pushed her face against the glass doors. "Because we need supplies and a place to sleep."

"There's still many hours until dark. We should use them."

Shadia turned to me, chewing her bottom lip for a moment before she sighed. "You're right. I still want a quick look, though."

"Why?"

"As I said, we need supplies. And if any place has a wheelchair, it's here."

"Oh. Good point."

I watched as she got my ax and used the blade to break the glass in the door. I might have argued that someone would hear us, and what if there were anyone inside the building, dead or alive? But I was pretty sure we would have heard them by now.

I waited as Shadia climbed through the door with my ax,

followed by the sound of more glass breaking. When the building swallowed the sound of her steps, I turned toward the road, keeping watch.

I looked through our bags until I found a pack of gum. I'd chewed through a lot of it while André was sick, trying to relieve some stress, but had managed to squirrel away one last pack in Shadia's rucksack. I found it now and popped a stick in my mouth.

Those were some of the longest minutes in my life, but finally, the sound of footsteps from within the building reached me, shortly followed by Shadia backing out the doors, pulling something after her.

"This view is ass-some!" I said as I looked at her behind.

She turned and stuck her tongue out at me before finally pulling a wheelchair through the doorway. It was a community chair with a red steel skeleton and thin, black fabric to form the seat. Shadia had filled it with stuff, and some of that stuff looked like pillows. She was keeping something behind her back, out of my sight, and I leaned over to try to get a look.

"What is that?" I asked as she turned on the brakes for the chair, turning her body to hide the object.

"A gift." Her grin was scaring me.

"What kind of gift?"

"Close your eyes."

"Sha?"

"Come on! Just do it." I did as she asked and almost jumped out of my skin when I felt her hands remove the bandana from around my face. Then she pushed something on top of my head, and my world grew a little darker. "OK, open them."

I did so, immediately seeing the rim of a hat at the top of my vision. "You found a hat?" I asked, reaching up to touch it.

"Yes. It's not as edgy as yours, but it's still a hat that will shade you from the sun. Don't make that face." Her grin grew even wider as my hands moved around the hat and felt what I was pretty sure were silk flowers. "You look so cute! Now, let me help you up so we can get moving."

I looked at the things in the chair. There was a closed bag of something, another ax, and two pillows.

"You brought another ax?" I asked.

"Thought it might be smart if we had one each. Just in case."

I grinned up at her, and Shadia rolled her eyes and pulled away from the bag. "Just get in your chair, granny."

"Oy!" I grabbed one of the pillows and tried to hit her, but she jumped back with a giggle. Mock-scowling, I put the pillow back into place.

The chair was sharp and uncomfortable, way too wide for me, and the armrests too high. We did what we could with the armrests, and the pillows filled in the leftover space and helped support me, but it only made me miss my own chair. It had become a part of me, had given me so much freedom. To just leave it behind like that ... it made me strangely sad.

As we got ready to leave, we took a look at the map, noticing that we would reach a town if we continued on this road. There was a chance it wasn't as bad as Oslo had been, but we didn't want to risk it, especially with us being more tired now. So we decided on a back road. It would take somewhat longer, but would keep us away from any big settlements for a little while, so in theory, we should be safe.

We'd spent almost an hour at the retirement home before Shadia gripped the handles of my chair and we moved out, leaving the building a little emptier than when we found it. I noticed that I didn't feel bad about stealing this stuff. While it hadn't been a big problem for me to begin with, I didn't care at all now. I wondered if Shadia cared. She'd always been the more law-abiding of us, but she showed no sign of regret. She did what she had to do to survive, and my respect for her grew even more.

By nightfall, we were both exhausted and practically asleep on our feet. I actually did fall asleep a couple of times. Shadia let me slumber, but by the time I woke up, we'd slowed to a crawl. Ahead, a white farmhouse surrounded by tired cars stood alone in the dark, and we agreed to use the house for the night. Shadia didn't even bother knocking, but walked around and ruined the back door to get us inside. We left the wheelchair outside, hidden among the other scrap in the garden before she carried me and our stuff inside, and we passed out on the empty bed in what must have once been a guestroom and office to whoever lived here before. They didn't need it now.

Excerpt from Medical Notebook

Through some mutation, the worm has two brains. One focuses on eating and keeping it alive through instinct, and one has a much more sinister plot in mind.

As it grows, the second brain moves the back end of the worm slowly and steadily along the esophagus. When it reaches the mouth, it moves to drill its way into the spine. This is when the flu symptoms start, as the body tries to fight it off. When reaching the brain, it somehow takes control of the subject. How, we never learned.

Meanwhile, the bottom half feeds on the flesh its twin provides and continues to lay eggs. These eggs make it to the mouth through the bloodstream, which continues to flow through some manipulation of the worm. When a host bites another host, the eggs move into it.

If the host is dead, the eggs die with it, but if the host survives the bite, the eggs hatch, and the process starts all over again.

We didn't know that in the beginning.

26

There were some simple food-stuffs at the farm that we ate for breakfast before leaving. Besides stealing the food, we also took the big knife that hung on the wall by the fireplace. Shadia thought I needed a knife, just in case I lost the ax.

We knew we had to pass through a town eventually, but we wanted to avoid it as much as possible. So, with the map in my lap, we headed along a forest road. Every now and again, the woods would give way to fields of wheat or corn, then a farmhouse in the distance. It was a weird experience, seeing these areas that were usually bustling with life this time of year stand so still and quiet. There were no zombies in our path. Most people had gone to town for help before they died, or died in their beds in closed up houses. It only made the lonely feeling hanging over us even heavier.

Around lunchtime, we had to turn onto a more maintained road that led to the freeway. We'd discussed how to avoid the big-ish town, but neither of us could think of anything. We had to keep to the better roads, or the uneven ground might bring on another seizure. The humping and dumping made me chew through my pain pills like they were candy, and my hands kept shaking on and off.

After eating, we headed into the sunlight and toward a more populated area. To get to the road we wanted, we had to walk across the freeway. Seeing as we were still pretty close to Oslo, there was a fair bet the road would be crowded with cars, making it hard to cross, and we were both on edge.

Houses appeared along the road, some still with cars in their driveways. I closed my eyes, listening. I told myself it was for the sound of shuffling feet, but really it was for the scraping of claws on doors and the whining of dogs. I didn't think cats would have any trouble getting out, but dogs couldn't use windows in the same way. Max had burned himself into my memory, and I couldn't help but think that other dogs were in the same situation. But there was no sound of scrabbling claws, no whines or howls, so I opened my eyes after a while. Even if they were safe from the parasite, they would have died of thirst a long time ago.

Shadia must have sensed my sadness, for she squeezed my shoulder with one hand without stopping. I leaned my chin against her hand before she pulled it back and sped up a little. The wind blew the scent of rot in our direction.

Finally, we found the crossing point, which thankfully turned out to be a tunnel running beneath the freeway. The road would bring us into a much more populated area, but for now, it was one obstacle less for us to deal with.

We followed the road until we could see houses rising ahead. The scent of rot was stronger now. We both wanted to move on, but neither of us wanted to traverse a town in the dark, not knowing where the sick had gone or where they might have died, so Shadia picked a house for us to spend the night in.

The house was a small, squat two-story building, and Shadia

left me in the driveway while she headed around to find a way in. It turned out there was no other door, so she broke a window and climbed inside, using me as a step-ladder to do so.

Sitting in the driveway, alone, I gripped my ax and scanned the street. We'd seen no sign of Nicholas or his men since they burned us out, and we could only hope they'd given up on us and gone back home. Not that we had any idea what we would do if we saw them again. I didn't think we would be lucky enough to run away a third time, and I didn't like relying on luck. The other option was to fight, but that only made me more afraid. I could still taste Nicholas's blood in my mouth when I thought about him. I felt how it was to cleave through a living person's arm with my ax, and hear his screams and the sudden thud of the blade hitting bone. The memories made my stomach turn, and my eyes warm with unshed tears.

The scent of rot was even stronger now, and I pulled up my bandana for some cover before I rolled to the door and used the handle of the ax to knock. I didn't want to yell for Shadia in case there were any zombies nearby that could hear me. We still didn't know how they tracked us, and I didn't want to take any chances.

Finally, Shadia unlocked the door and pulled me inside, chair and all. The house smelled of mildew and some kind of animal musk. There was a layer of dust everywhere, so thick that everything was grey except for Shadia's footsteps, leaving clear proof of her passage.

"There's a basement," she said. "I think we should sleep there tonight."

I didn't argue. The steadily growing smell was making me jumpy, and I wanted to be as out of sight as I could. Shadia locked the door and pushed an old telephone-bench in front of it before she rolled me into the kitchen and showed me the trapdoor leading into the basement.

"This isn't a basement," I said after she'd helped me down the ladder. "It's a root cellar."

The room was barely two-by-two meters, with shelves set against the walls, making it even smaller. Shadia and I would have to spoon to fit. There were no windows, and the walls and floor were made of dirt. The only light was the fading sunlight seeping through the cracks in the floor above. And this room was as dusty as everything else. I swear I could feel the grime settle on my skin.

"Is there a difference?" Shadia asked as she climbed up the ladder again.

"Well, a basement usually has windows!" I called up after her. "And their walls and floor aren't just hard dirt. What's to say the walls won't cave in on us?"

"They haven't yet, right?" She dropped our sleeping bags down the opening in the ceiling.

"No."

"Then stop fussing. It's cute, but this is what we get for now. Make do, *habibi*."

"Make do, *habibi*," I mumbled under my breath.

"What did you say?"

"Nothing."

"M-hm."

With my chair hidden away, Shadia climbed down and closed the trap door. There was no use in trying to hide my chair, as the marks in the dust would give us away if anyone thought to enter the house, but Shadia didn't seem to care. She was still afraid of Nicholas, and who could blame her?

We made the best of the small space, using a headlamp for light and unrolling one sleeping bag along the floor and another above. The rucksacks would have to do as pillows.

We helped each other clean up with wipes and antibacterial gel. Luckily, Shadia's period was over, which made cleaning a lot easier for her.

Dinner was cold canned peas, not something I'd recommend to my worst enemy. Afterwards, we chewed a stick of gum each before spitting the rubbery candy into the cans, undressing, and lying together between the sleeping bags. I wanted to explore the content of the shelves, which were filled with glass jars and small boxes, but was too tired. Not that Shadia would let me explore anyway, even if she herself stayed awake to read a little.

I was almost asleep when a sound reached me. It wasn't loud, more of a steady hum. I wasn't even sure Shadia heard it before she put her Kindle away and crawled deeper into the sleeping bags.

"What's that?" I whispered.

She buried her nose in my neck. "Don't know."

We lay in silence, listening to the sound. Then came a moan. Weak, but there. The sound must have floated to us from the street and slipped through the broken window, the thin walls, and the cracks in our ceiling. With the shuffling and the scent of rot that I'd almost gotten used to by now, it pointed to zombies. But how could we hear a zombie walking?

Something thudded against the side of the house, making us both jump.

After another thump, Shadia moved.

"What're you doing?" I whispered, grabbing for her in the dark but missing.

"Going to check."

"No!" It was a hiss, but the sound was so loud. I held my breath as I watched the shadow of Shadia move away from me and stand.

"I'll be right back, *habibi*."

"Shadia!"

"I'll be right back."

With that, she climbed the ladder and snuck out through the trapdoor, letting it close behind her and leaving me alone in the dark.

27

Holding my breath, I listened to Shadia's footsteps as they walked across the floor above and headed into the hallway, where there was a window looking out onto the street. The window she'd broken was also in the hallway, but it looked into the wall of the garage building beside it, hiding it from view if someone threw a casual glance at the house.

As her footsteps grew distant, the thudding increased, followed by more moans. Another thud, then another, until they overlapped and seemed to grow into one sound.

Shadia's steps came running across the floor, and she threw open the trapdoor. Almost falling down the ladder, she pulled the trapdoor closed with a thud that was so loud I drew a shuddering breath.

"What is it?" I asked, voice barely audible over the thudding from above, the moaning, and a scraping sound that made my teeth itch.

Shadia didn't answer; she just sat on the dirt floor by my feet. I couldn't see her face, but I could hear her ragged breathing.

"Hey," I whispered.

When she still didn't answer, I moved. Crawling, I made my way to her and found that she was shaking. Wrapping my arms around her, I drew her close. One of her hands flew up and clutched at my shirt, the other covering her mouth as she rested her forehead against my chin.

She continued gasping for breath, her body shaking and shivering in my arms, and I had no idea what to do. Cold sweat dampened her shirt so fast I was afraid there was a leak in the floor above us, but there was no other water. She wasn't crying. She was scared. So, so scared.

Above, the thudding continued, but the moaning started to die down.

We stayed like that for a long time. My back was aching from the position I was in, but I wouldn't let her go. The sweat on Shadia's back was almost dry before she spoke. Not moving, she whispered just loud enough for me to hear.

"Zombies everywhere. Filling the street. They're stuck on the fence beside the house. One of them keep walking into the and bouncing back. When I went to look, they noticed me. More and more of them turned away from the road and came for us. They were clawing on the walls. Trying to get in."

"It's OK," I said.

She pulled away from me, gripped my shoulders and shook me a little. "It's not. I drew them here, Kit. There's nowhere for us to go. They'll get in, and they'll get us, and it's my fault!"

Her voice was getting louder. Outside, the moans had stopped, although a thud came every now and again. I was afraid her voice would draw more zombies, so I slapped my hand over her mouth. Shadia gripped my wrist, her nails digging into my skin. My hand found the back of her neck and forced her head toward mine until our foreheads rested against each other. I could see the whites of her eyes as they jumped around in fear.

"We're OK," I said, and her eyes focused on mine. "They're not in yet. Listen, the moans have stopped. I don't think they know we're here."

Her grip on my wrist loosened, and I lowered my hand. She moved until her fingers were entwined with mine.

"But how?" she whispered. "I didn't make a sound up there, and they still noticed me. Then I make a sound down here, but they don't?"

"I don't know, but it seems they're not attracted by noise." I stopped whispering, talking in my usual voice. There were no moans from above, no more thudding or scraping. No sign the zombies knew we were here.

"So how?" Shadia asked, her hysterical voice calm now that she had something to think about.

"I don't know, but I think you should write this down. It's a discovery, even if we don't know what it means."

"Yes. Yes, that's a good idea. Do you think I can turn on a light?" Her voice was growing eager.

I nodded and leaned back, stifling a yawn. Shadia noticed despite my best efforts. Crawling to my side, she used her arms and body to lay us both down on the floor. She pulled the other sleeping bag up to cover us.

"I'll do it tomorrow," she said. "Now, we sleep."

I didn't think I could sleep with the sound of what I was sure was an army of undead walking past in my ears, but I was so tired after a day in the sun and this latest spike of adrenalin and fear, that I slipped into sleep soon enough.

"Hello everyone, and welcome to Skogli Rehabiliterings Senter. We are happy that you chose to stay here with us and let us help you with your situation."

I sank down in my chair, eyes heavy after the trip and body tired.

It didn't help that I hardly slept last night, worried about coming here.

"During the next four weeks, we will help you learn to know the limits of your body, understand what Myalgic Encephalomyelitis is, and how to best shape your everyday life according to this handicap."

My eye twitched at the word 'handicap', and I looked at the people standing at the end of the room. Two men and two women. They'd introduced themselves, but I'd forgotten their names. I did remember their roles, though. The man sitting to the far right, with dark grey hair, half-moon glasses, and a white frock, was the primary physician for our group. The woman sitting beside him was the 'teacher'. She was as grey-haired as the man but looked a lot friendlier. She would tell us how to handle our health issues, teach us its known history, and what little they knew about it. The woman talking was the shrink, blonde and young, but with a stern look in her eyes, and the leader of this department. The last man was our physical therapy contact. Where the other three were different shades of Norwegian pale skin, he had a beautiful brown tone to his, and his hair was almost black. He would be there to take care of us through mindfulness classes, swimming, and physical therapy. I'd heard two of the other women in the group talk about how hot he was, and that they wished they knew there would be men like him here so they could bring their good swimwear. I noticed that, compared to the three others, his eyes were the kindest.

"Now, we could give you a lot more information here, but we understand that you will be tired after a day of travel and taking in the new environment. Because of that, we will cut this meeting short. You have all gotten the keys to your rooms. If you haven't been in there yet, there is a folder on the desk with your schedule and information on the facilities. The evening meal will start in five minutes and last for ninty minutes, so you have time to take a

184

look at the folder before eating, if you wish. With that, we hope you have a pleasant stay here at Skogli, and that you have a good night. If you have any questions, feel free to come up and ask before the meal."

A silence fell over the room before people started moving. I couldn't help comparing us to a class at school waiting for the bell to ring.

There were eight of us in the group, only two men, and I was the youngest at twenty-four. The two women I'd heard talk about swimwear hurried up to the dark-skinned man. One of the two men in the group also went up, but probably to ask a question instead of to flirt. The rest of us filed out of the meeting room. While all the others moved toward the eating hall, I headed toward the elevator. I'd brought some food and would eat in my room tonight.

A primal scream ripped through the dream/memory, and my eyes flew open. The scream was cut short as moans from what sounded like a hundred zombie throats rose triumphantly in the air—if zombies could be triumphant.

Shadia's hand on my stomach started shaking, and her breathing was ragged again, growing more and more shallow every second.

"Hey," I whispered, turning around, so we were face to face. "It's OK."

She nodded but didn't answer, too focused on breathing to form words.

"Just breathe with me," I said, pressing my forehead to hers and breathing into her face. I was sorry for the possible bad breath I exposed her to, but not sorry when she matched her inhales and exhales with mine, calming.

We stayed like that until she fell back asleep. I didn't dare move into a more comfortable position. Instead, I stayed awake a little while, listening to the world.

The heavy shuffling was back, every now and again broken by a moan, and in-between all that, I was sure I heard them feeding on whatever they had killed outside. I was sure my hearing wasn't that good, but even if it was just my imagination making these sounds, it made me sweat from fear.

Finally, I matched my own breathing to Shadia's and fell into sleep again.

"So, what's this about?" I asked the doctor as Shadia and I took our seats, and he closed the door behind us.

Three weeks ago, the nurses at this clinic had poked and prodded me with needles after the doctor asked them to check everything. Apparently, he didn't want to take any chances with me, for which Shadia was grateful. I was just bored. Two weeks ago, I'd found another lump in the crook of my elbow. Much smaller than the one on the throat, but still there. One week ago, another doctor had cut out the lump on my throat to send for some kind of test, then taken the lump in my elbow as well when I told him about it. I didn't want to admit it, but I was starting to worry.

The doctor sat behind his desk and folded his hands on the tabletop. "Katerina," he said. "I am sorry to say this, but we think you have cancer."

Shadia gripped my hand.

"What?" I asked, not able to contain a smile. This had to be a joke, right?

"Well, the tests we've taken confirm that you have Hodgkins Lymphoma. There are still more tests needed to show how advanced it is, but I want you to know that the prognosis is very good with this type of cancer. I've already gotten in contact with the hospital regarding your ..."

His voice grew muffled as I stared at him. He was still speaking, but I couldn't hear him. All I heard was my own breathing, shallow, and afraid. Cancer. He said I had cancer. How could I have cancer? I was just twenty-two years old! I wasn't supposed to get sick. I ...

... forced myself awake, unable to handle the memory any longer. Blinking against the dark, I looked into Shadia's sleeping face.

The sounds, imaginary or not, from outside had quieted down. I couldn't hear any shuffling or moaning. Hopefully, the zombies had moved past, and we were safe for now–from the zombies, if not from our own memories.

Hardly a week after that conversation with the doctor, another doctor told me I had stage three lymphoma. I didn't need surgery, but the treatment was aggressive. I got really sick and almost died twice from the treatment alone. It was hell on Shadia and my family. It was hell on me. Then, just over a year after we started treatment, I was in remission. My health had gone downhill ever since.

Not wanting to think about it, I cuddled closer to Shadia, hoping she would wake, but she stayed asleep, exhausted. Instead of waking her, I drew in her smell, sweaty and stale as it was, and tried to think about something else, anything else.

When I fell asleep again, I was thinking about our life at the cabin. How we would live off the land and be happy. Just the two of us. I didn't remember any dreams when I woke up again.

28

We only saw one zombie the next day: a straggler with both legs missing. One was chewed off at the knee, the other at the hip.

As far as I could tell, zombies didn't eat dead meat, so the woman crawling on the road in front of us must have been alive when her legs were eaten. Was she like me? Someone bound to a wheelchair or crutches to help move around? Was that how the zombies got to that part of her? Her legs dragged behind for some reason? I couldn't imagine how it must have been to lie there, having zombies chew on you.

The thought made me shiver, and I forced it away. This would not be my fate.

We put her out of her misery and moved on, a heavy silence hanging over us.

At lunchtime, we were in the parking lot of Lier Mall and agreed on spending the night there. It, and all the other malls, had been closed up as the sickness hit, when there weren't enough people to keep them open, much less go shopping. Despite that, I had seen people saying online they would meet at the malls to survive the zombies. It didn't look like anyone had done that here, thankfully.

Breaking in through one of the many front doors, we made

our way through the empty mall, listening to the echo of Shadia's footsteps. All the shops were hidden behind plastic shutters, but they didn't stand much chance against my ax when we found a furniture store. There, we found ourselves a good king-sized bed with silken sheets and a bunch of fluffy pillows to spend the night. After, Shadia found a bookstore, of course.

She read me to sleep that night, after a calm afternoon spent searching the mall for things we might need. We topped up on our medications and got some new camping gear, and Shadia got some new clothes. I grabbed a few cotton t-shirts, as the ones I'd brought were smelly and nasty by now. Shadia teased me for staying with grey and black, and I countered with having to be a raincloud so her rainbow could survive. That earned me a kiss. We also splurged on chocolate from one of the posher shops.

The next day, we emerged from the mall before the sun was up, both having woken on our own, ready to set out. The sky was overcast with fluffy white clouds, but the sky on the horizon was dark. When we saw this, we stopped by a grocery store and found plastic zip lock bags to wrap around the things in our not-so-waterproof messenger bags, hoping to keep it all dry. Outside, a brisk wind had picked up and blew in our faces, threatening to take my hat with it. After Shadia caught it three times, we tied it down with a scarf from our new winter gear.

The road entered a forest and kept to it for most of the day. The only time we saw something other than trees was when they gave way to a great lake, and when we reached what must have been the origin of the horde. It used to be a motocross-track, but the military had put up fences, and the track was hidden away by tents. There was blood soaked into the sand, and the smell of death still lingered in the air, so we passed by as fast as possible.

We ate our lunch and an early dinner in the shade of tall trees, with the wind getting brisker and brisker for every meter we walked. As the sun began to set, we saw a clearing in the road ahead, which turned out to be a hamlet of houses and a kindergarten.

By now, the wind was so cold we both wore jackets and were huddled into ourselves, not wanting to bring out the rest of the winter gear in case we would boil in their confines.

Compared to the other kindergartens we'd seen, this one was empty; all its occupants probably hid somewhere at the motocross-track. I wondered if a zombie baby even stood a chance at surviving, or if the other zombies would kill it before it had a turned.

The day grew steadily grayer, the air pressing down on us, promising a storm, but the darkest clouds were still a bit off. We walked as far as we could that day, afraid the weather would hinder our progress later.

The storm hit that night, and we spent two days in a house, waiting the worst of it out. It was still raining on the third day, but the wind had died down, and we hadn't seen any lightning or heard any thunder in almost a full day, so we dared leave the safety of the building behind and set out, hidden beneath the raingear we'd found at the mall.

We'd reached the outskirt of Drammen before the storm hit, and now we wanted to get through and out the other side. To get across the river, we could either follow the clogged freeway or take the other bridges, but these led straight into the city. We opted for the city, hoping most of the zombies had joined the horde Shadia had seen—she swore it had been big enough to hold the whole city and more.

No such luck.

Despite the rain, the zombies came. They were dripping wet, both from the rain and from decomposition, but there were so many of them, and they were everywhere.

We did well getting through the Northside of town, killing those that came too close and leaving those we could behind. We should have killed them all.

29

The bridge was two lanes wide and blessedly empty of cars. There'd been a roadblock a few streets back, forcing cars to head up onto the freeway, where they stood still and empty, like in Oslo. The river rushed beneath us, swollen and still swelling from the heavy rain.

The bridge led onto a small island, and it wasn't until we were halfway across it we realized something was wrong.

Because of the rain, the visibility was poor, and we both kept our heads down to keep the water out of our eyes. We hadn't given much thought to the improvised fence at the mouth of the bridge, open as it was, but as we passed two more, we started to realize something was up.

When the third netting fence came into view, Shadia stopped.

"Sha?" I asked, turning to look up at her and getting an eyeful of water.

"I think we should go back," she answered, not taking her eyes off the murky world ahead.

"Take the freeway?"

She looked at me. "Yes, or find a boat or something, but we shouldn't be here."

"Agreed," I answered, dropping my head and letting the

water drip off my hat. I was scanning the bridge ahead, sure I saw movement, but it was hard to tell.

"Then we go back," Shadia said and turned us around.

We were by the second roadblock when we saw them. The zombies we'd left behind were shambling across the bridge toward us. They were slow—we could easily outrun them—but they were many. We could see them pushed up against the wire of the fence, just a few slipping through the opening at a time, but there was no chance we could fight our way through them all. They filled the bridge, making a roadblock of their own.

Without a word, Shadia turned us around and jogged across the bridge.

We saw clear movement in the haze ahead. More zombies heading our way, rattling the fences, as one or two at a time slipped through the openings.

"Shit," I mumbled as Shadia cursed in Arabic. "What do we do now?"

My heartbeat echoed in my ears as I watched another zombie slip through the fence ahead.

"We survive," Shadia said, overpowering the sound of my heart, but she couldn't disguise the small shake in her own voice.

I turned to see she'd left me, sprinting to the last fence we'd passed. Two zombies were already at it, pushing against the metal. Shadia paid them no mind and grabbed at the links, pulling and pushing. The metal screamed against the asphalt before it gave and clanged shut.

"That should give us some time," she said as she jogged back.

"So, what? We fight our way through?" I asked, indicating the throng in front of us.

"Do you have a better idea, *habibi*?"

"No."

"Then we fight."

Before I could answer, she bent down, pulled down my bandana, and kissed me. I kissed her back, gripping the back of her head to pull her closer. Inhaling her scent, I let it fill me: jasmine and books and *her*. Pulling back, she leaned her forehead against mine and stared into my eyes.

"Stay alive, OK?" I said.

She swallowed and blinked. "You too."

I grinned, trying to turn my fear into bravery. "Always."

She made a sound like a half-chuckle, half-sob before she kissed my nose lightly. "I love you."

My grin dying, I kissed her nose just as lightly. "I love you too."

With that, she stood and pulled her ax from its resting place on her back, pulled up her bandana to cover mouth and nose, and started walking toward the zombies.

I stared after her for a moment, not sure what to do or say or even think. Then I made sure all the bags I carried were out of the way but secured to my body, that my knife was within easy reach, and that there was nothing in the way of the wheels. No way was I letting her face this alone. I pushed forward, happy that the slick surface gave me extra speed as I reached Shadia, and buried my ax in the head of the first zombie to reach us.

Shadia yelled that I cheated as she passed by and took out another. Then they were upon us, and I couldn't keep an eye on her anymore. All I could do was fight the grasping hands, the clicking jaws, the heavy bodies as they fell over me.

Always hit the head, for if they went down and were still alive, they could topple me over. I couldn't move much, the bodies blocking my wheels, so I let them come to me, steadily moving me backwards and away from Shadia without either of us noticing.

There was blood everywhere. My hands were slick on the shaft of the ax despite my padded gloves. The rain kept dripping in my eyes, having soaked through my hat and hair. It was in the way, but I didn't dare remove it. The bandana kept the blood from my mouth and nose, and my glasses and hat kept the blood from my eyes. I'd long since lost count of how many I'd taken down. All I saw was gray flesh and maggots moving in open mouths and eye sockets.

The scream of metal made me look up for a second to see the fence in front of us bending, letting more zombies flood through. We'd almost cleared the area, and the thought of fighting more made my heart sink. I was panting, already exhausted. I wasn't sure I could lift the ax to swing even once more.

A zombie came from the side and slammed into me. It looked a lot fresher than most of those I'd taken out. Its skin was grey, yes, but the flesh hadn't started falling off the bone, and there were no maggots that I could see. He wore hiking gear, and part of my mind thought he might have been a survivor. Like us. Maybe the same one who had opened the gates we'd passed through on the bridge. Both his arms were missing, chewed away to the bone before the zombies lost interest in him. Despite being fresher, he was still dead and rotting, and not strong enough to topple me over, but he was strong enough to push me.

I slammed into the side of the bridge and screamed in fear. He was too close for me to use the ax, so I tried to push it away with one hand while I reached for my knife with the other.

Another zombie rushed forward, finding his way under my arm and slamming into my chest. I toppled to the side, feeling cold metal against the lower part of my back. Another zombie came from the side, and I lifted one leg, kicking at it. Too late, I realized the movement pushed me backwards further, and there was nothing there to stop me from falling.

30

For a heartbeat, time stopped. I hung in the air, seeing a zombie try to follow me over the edge of the bridge but getting stuck on something. I saw it reach out its arms for me. I saw my own hand gripping my ax and realized it might hurt me if I didn't get rid of it. The pink of my glove was visible through the dark blood of the dead. I felt the rain hit my face and lips like tiny needles, and my glasses and hat loosening. I heard the roar of the river, Shadia screaming my name, and the flapping of my raincoat around me. I met the zombie's black eyes.

The heartbeat was over, and time rushed back in.

Turning in the air, I flung my arm to the side, letting go of the ax. It had barely left my fingers when I slapped into the water. The skin along my hip and shoulder prickle in pain. Then I was pulled under, and it was so cold I gasped, swallowing water. I forced myself not to cough as I was tumbled and spun by the stream.

Opening my eyes, I saw only darkness and rushing muck. Something tugged at my shoulder, and I grabbed at it, finding my messenger bag. Hugging it to my chest, I curled into a ball, making myself as small as possible, praying I wouldn't hit anything.

My head broke the surface, and I let the coughs go. Something big and dark rushed past, but by the time I'd turned to see what it was, it was swallowed by the rain.

The current tugged at me again, and I was barely able to pull in a breath and close my mouth before I was under again.

I knew enough not to fight the stream. Knew that it would win if I tried, and I would only exhaust myself faster. It was hard though, just letting it pull me away from Shadia. The water was cold, and I was tired. My fingers started twitching where they grabbed at the messenger bag, and my lungs started screaming.

It felt like The Fog was just at the edge of my mind, but I knew that wasn't the case. This time, it was because of a lack of oxygen, which was much worse.

My tumbling grew drowsy, and I opened my eyes again. This time, salt stung them.

I was still held by the stream, but I must have reached the ocean, where it was much less dangerous. Hope bloomed in my chest, and I wanted to swim, but I wasn't sure which way was up or down. Forcing myself to stay calm, I let one bubble out of my mouth. It was instantly grabbed by the current, but not before I felt it slip to the side of my mouth. That way was up, then.

Following the the current, I tumbled around until I was turned the right way. My ears popped and my nose was stuffed with water, but I knew where to go now.

Using one hand to keep the messenger bag at my side, I started swimming. My clothes and boots and bag were heavy, and it felt like they were pulling me down, like I couldn't reach the surface with them all still on, but I knew I couldn't let any of it go. The bag held my medication and food, and I needed my shoes and clothing to keep warm when I got out of the water.

My hand broke the surface. Cold wind and rain bit into it, making it twitch and curl into itself. I hoped it was just from the cold, not a seizure coming.

My head finally broke through, and I spat out murky water and gasped down fresh air. When my breathing calmed, I shook water from my eyes and slowly turned around. The world was misty from the rain, and the grey ocean kept buffeting me from every direction, trying to exhaust me and pull me under again, but I didn't let it. I turned and turned until I finally saw something dark on the horizon. That must be land.

Still hugging the bag to my chest, I started swimming. It was hard swimming with only one arm and my legs, but I didn't dare let the bag go.

My teeth were chattering, I was so cold, and my legs kept jumping this way and that as I pulled them in and out, in and out. Even my arm wanted to dance, but I forced it on course as much as I could.

I kept my eyes on the black, not listening to the voice inside me saying it was too far away, that I'd never make it. I'd made it this far. I would get to the shore and onto land. I would not drown.

The Fog was creeping at the edges of my mind, and more than once, I found that I had stopped swimming, or let the bag slip from my grip, or just plain started sinking. Every time I forced The Fog back, but it got harder and harder.

By the time I reached land, I'd forgotten what I was swimming toward. I just knew I had to keep swimming. When my hand touched the rock, I almost continued swimming right into it. Instead, some instinct took over, and I grabbed it.

I tried climbing out, but a wave almost pulled me out with it. Sheer stubbornness and survival instinct made me keep my grip on the rock. When another wave rushed in, I used it to lift me onto land. When it pulled back, I was finally out of the water.

Crawling on all fours, dragging the messenger bag behind me, every limb jerking and threatening to let go beneath me, I made my way away from the water and onto the shore.

When I was sure the waves wouldn't get to me anymore, I fell down and let my arms and legs go.

* * *

When I woke from The Fog, my limbs were still twitching, and my back kept jerking. It hurt, but I wasn't sure I could move. I slipped into The Fog again. When I came to next, only my back was jerking. I was starting to feel warm, despite the chill rain falling on me, and the ocean water soaked into my clothes.

A little part of my mind knew that the heat wasn't good; knew that I had to find somewhere dry and get out of these clothes. Most of me didn't want to. I just wanted to stay where I was and sleep. I was so tired and sore. I didn't want to do this anymore. But the part that knew the heat was bad was too stubborn, and somehow I found myself pushing up enough to look around.

I could see a shadow that looked like a mountain or a tall slope right ahead. Closer around me were rocks and more rocks, as well as small shrubs. There was nowhere dry nearby.

Again, I considered just lying down and letting The Fog take me, but before I'd had a chance to decide, I was pushing up on all fours again. My muscles vibrated, wanting to shake again. Instead of listening to them, I started crawling.

I kept my head down and focused on breathing steadily, supplying my body with oxygen. I only glanced up every now and again to make sure I was still moving forward. My crawling was slow going, and the first ten times or so I looked up, I only saw rocks and shrubs. The next time however, there was another shadow in the rain.

Primal fear roared through me. For a moment, I froze in place. Fear pumped fresh adrenalin through my veins, which pushed The Fog further into my mind–not far, but enough for me to think clearly. That shadow wasn't a zombie but looked to be something bigger.

Moving faster, I neared the shadow and soon saw that it was an upturned boat. It probably wasn't dry, but at least it was out of the rain.

With frost-numb limbs, I crawled to the boat and started moving around it, using my hands to explore as much as my eyes. Finally, I found an opening I could fit through.

I shimmied and kicked until I was under the boat, then I willingly sunk into The Fog.

Excerpt from Medical Notebook

The worm's complete control isn't final until some time after rigor mortis. The theory is that this happens to give the other worms in the stomach and blood time to die. The worm nestled in the brain is able to feed off it, and in that way, integrate itself into the central nervous system.

When reanimating the body, the second brain now moves it to hunt for meat, be it human or animal; it doesn't care, as long as it is fresh.

31

I woke in sporadic bursts after that.

The first time, I undressed down to my underwear, flinging the wet clothes away. I was clear enough to notice that the dry grass was sharp and kept poking at me before I disappeared into The Fog again.

The second time, I was able to find a somewhat better sleeping position, one that didn't involve my limbs slamming into the sides of the boat as they jerked and danced.

The third time, I managed to take a painkiller and dry swallow it, not trusting my shaking hand not to throw the water bottle away if I tried to drink.

When I woke the fourth time, my shakes had mostly disappeared, and I was dry. The rain was still drumming against the boat hull, but it was lighter now. I lay awake a little while, listening to the rain and the ocean outside before I fell into a somewhat more natural sleep.

I don't know how long that sleep lasted. When I woke again, there was only a faint vibration in my muscles. A warning that the seizure was calming down, but could still come back. The Fog was still in the back of my mind, but not threatening to take over again. I didn't want to risk doing too much, but I also knew that something had to be done.

Moving slowly, I was able to drink a little water from one of my bottles, and eat a few nuts. That was enough for my hands to begin shaking and hurting again, so I took another painkiller and went back to sleep.

This was the routine for the next few times I woke up. Force down some water, nuts, and a painkiller, then go back to sleep. I think I noticed the light seeping beneath the boat changing, and the rain changed to a whisper, the wind almost dying completely. Even with my watch waking me every morning and every evening, I wasn't sure how much time passed. I went to the bathroom once, crawling into the rain and to the other end of the boat, where I relieved myself. After that one time, I didn't eat or drink enough to have anything to waste. I think I'd been under that boat for almost five days when I woke and was clearheaded enough to consider what had happened and what to do next.

The first thing I did was take inventory. My watch was still functioning, which was good. I'd barely been awake enough to know if I took the right pill, but it had been enough to keep me alive, it seemed. My clothes were long since dry, even if they were crusted in salt. I was running low on both food and water, as the bag only held so much. It did hold a set of clothes, kept dry in large zip lock bags, which I now pulled on. The salt made my skin itch. The knife Shadia had made me take was still on my belt in its sheath. I thanked whoever invented hunting-knives with straps to make sure they wouldn't fall out. This meant I had a weapon. And I had more than enough medication, but it wouldn't last forever, so I needed to find Shadia. She would have the rest. But how?

As I pondered the question, I fell asleep again. Taking inventory had clearly been too taxing. When I woke again, the light hadn't changed much, and I knew where I had to go. Before we left André's place, we'd agreed to meet at the closest train station if we were separated.

My first thought was of the station in Drammen, but I pushed it aside. No way was I going back there again. But where was the next one? I didn't know, as I'd never taken the train down this way, but I was pretty sure the line ran along the ocean. In theory, I should be able to find the track and just follow it South to the next station. Hopefully, Shadia would be there, waiting for me. I didn't want to consider what it would mean if she wasn't there.

Instead of thinking about the what-ifs, I started preparing for the journey. It was slow going, as any movement hurt, and I ended up taking a multitude of naps, but finally, I thought I was ready.

When the alarm on my clock woke me the next morning, I started by taking in the bottles I'd let stand outside in the rain to fill up. The rain had become a drizzle now, leaving the bottles half-full, but that would have to do. Carrying two full bottles would probably be too heavy for me anyway. I'd slept in my clothes, hoping to limber them up a little, so all that was left was to pull on my boots. After that, I pulled on the messenger bag, fastening it around my waist with my belt to make sure it would not get in the way, then I grabbed the two pieces of wood I'd hacked loose from the boat with my knife. I tied them over my knees using the one bandage that had been in my bag. I did the same with two smaller pieces of wood on my hands but kept the bandage loose enough that I could pull my hands free fast if I needed to. Finally, I pulled on my raincoat and put on the spare sunglasses from my messenger bag.

After a short rest, I left the safety of the boat.

The world wasn't as hazy as I had feared, and with the protection of the wood pieces, the crawling wasn't as painful as it could have been. It was still slow going, as I often had to rest, and I hurt a lot from the position I was in.

Noon came with a change in scenery. The stony ground turned to a path running between stiff, high grass. It was well-trodden and had probably been popular with people going to the ocean.

I rested at the mouth of the path, giving myself an hour of lying curled up partly under a bush and just breathing. My muscles were vibrating, but not shaking. The rest helped, and when I was sure I could move without triggering further vibrations, I took another painkiller and drank what was left of my cola. I should probably have saved it, but I needed to find the tracks before dark. From there, it shouldn't be far to the next station, and they probably had cola I could drink there—not to mention food.

Thoughts of food on my mind, I started crawling up the path. I wasn't hungry, but I knew a meal would do me good. I had two bags of jerky in my bag, but I hadn't dared to touch them. Who knew how many zombie-worm eggs I'd swallowed in the river? Or might have come down with the rain I'd been drinking since? I thanked the stars I'd been clear enough those first days not to eat the jerky, or I might not have been crawling along now.

That thought gave my stubbornness an extra boost, and we crawled on, my stubbornness and me.

As the gray light of day started to turn to night, houses appeared out of the gloom.

The path had let up to a parking lot, empty and quiet, and

from there, I found a road to follow, hoping it would take me to the train station. But no, it had taken me into a neighborhood instead. I sniffed as tears of frustration and fear started rolling down my cheeks, mixing with the rain.

If I didn't find the tracks soon, there was no saying what would happen. Or, there was, but I didn't want to think about it. I'd crawled across a smaller road on the way here. I could go back to that and hope it led to the station, but if I hadn't found the tracks by now, I was sure they must be further inland. Either way, I wasn't sure I could handle turning back right now. Not when I was so tired, and my mind felt a little like it was breaking. As best I could, I crawled into the neighborhood.

The houses that rose around me were big and well kept, with large yards and probably too many rooms to count. Some of the houses even had stone lions guarding their driveway.

Without giving it much thought, I crawled into the first driveway I reached. It held a double garage on one side and a huge white house in the middle, with three broad stone steps leading to the front door.

I crawled up and leaned my back against the door, breathing and crying a little more. I was maxed out on the strong painkillers, but as I sat there and watched the last of the light disappear, I took a Paracet, hoping it would bolster my regular meds.

When my breathing grew shallow and relaxed and my eyelids were so heavy I could hardly keep them open anymore, I turned and knocked on the door. No one answered or moved on the inside, so I tried the knob. The door was locked–no surprise there.

Pulling myself to my knees, I used one of the plank-pieces to break the flimsy window beside the doorknob. It had a sticker on it claiming there was a house alarm, but I didn't think anyone would come to check why the alarm had been triggered, if it was triggered at all. Alarms needed power, right?

After cleaning out the splinters of glass with the plank-piece, I reached inside and turned the knob. The door opened without a sound, and I crawled inside, kicking it shut behind me.

The Fog was creeping closer and closer, but somehow I locked the door behind me and crawled deeper into the house, finding a small bathroom first.

I undressed to my underwear, leaving my clothes in a wet heap on the marble floor, and managed to stand and turn on the taps. There was still water in the pipes here as well, so I washed my hands and arms with a rose-scented soap before I stole some of the mouthwash standing in one of the cabinets. I pushed the bottle into my bag before I used one of the plush towels to dry off. A fleece robe hung on the inside of the door, and I shuffled into it before I sank down to the floor again.

Cleaning up had been such an automatic action that The Fog had moved to the back of my mind again. Able to think a little clearer, I started looking around and soon found the kitchen.

I looked through the lower cabinets and the part of the fridge that I could reach without standing up. It was full of vegetables and containers of prepared food, some of it still looking edible, not to mention the whole inside of the door was full of bottles of different flavored sparkling water. Most of them were unopened. I pulled out all the containers and opened them one after another, finding mostly vegetarian meals.

Taking one of the big bottles of sparkly water and a box of

fried noodles and greens that still looked OK with me into the living room. I crawled onto the soft sofa, pulled a furry blanket over my cold limbs, and started eating.

When I almost fell asleep while chewing, I put the container on the glass table and curled up, falling asleep almost before I'd found a good position.

32

I woke at nine p.m. from my alarm and had to look around a little to find my bag. I'd left it at the foot of the sofa, but it took me a moment of panic to remember. With my long-term meds in my stomach, I forced down two mouthfuls of rice and vegetables and drank from the water bottle. It was big and heavy for me to move, so I soon put it down, cap just barely on, and fell asleep again.

I slept right through the night and didn't remember taking my evening or morning meds. Instead, I woke just after noon, and it took me a moment to remember where I was.

After eating and drinking a little more and doing my stuff in the bathroom, I started looking around the house. I didn't even pretend to consider going upstairs, but there was more than enough for me to see on the ground floor.

I found a washing room with freshly folded clothes and looked through them until I found a pair of jeans, socks, and a cotton long-sleeve t-shirt I thought would fit me and not itch too much. Anything had to be better than the salt-crusted fabrics I'd left in the bathroom. Leaving the robe behind, I dressed in my new finds. They were all a little too big, but considering the fabrics were mostly new to me, that wasn't a problem. If they'd been tighter, I might have had trouble with them itching or hurting my sensitive skin. I wouldn't have minded a new set of underwear either, but no matter how freshly clean they were, I would not use the underwear of someone else. No way, no how.

I'd noticed a bunch of boy's clothes while I looked, and snooping around some more proved that a teenage boy had lived here. In the hallway, I found well-used sneakers, and a school bag in the kitchen. The tab on the inside said 'Christopher', but I tried to forget that as soon as I saw it. In the living room, I found a bunch of DVDs for teenagers and some for adults. It was a big collection, and if there had been any power, I might have let myself forget about the real world and follow Batman as he fought the Joker. In the bathroom I'd used earlier, I found anti-acne cream and a lot of hair products. Looking in the mirror, I let my hair out of its tired braid and was almost shocked to see the green locks fall around my face. It felt like I'd dyed it in a whole other life. Using my dry-shampoo, I tried to clean it as well as I could and had to evacuate the bathroom because of the smell of the chemicals.

I found a new flashlight, batteries, painkillers, canned food, and matches, but no chewing gum. I missed gum.

It was almost dinner-time before I found what I was actually looking for. It was hidden in one of the drawers in the kitchen, lying beneath recipes and calendars and phonebooks: a small book of the area for tourists. Flipping it open, I found multiple maps inside.

Almost weeping with relief, I made my way into the living room again and curled up on the sofa. While forcing down a little more of the fried rice, I flipped through the book in the fading light until I found what I thought must be a map of the area. According to the map, the closest station was Galleberg, but it looked impossibly far away. The good thing was that it seemed to be in the middle of nowhere, only small towns around it, so there shouldn't be many zombies.

I marked the page and slipped the book into one of the many zip-lock bags in my bag. Still eating, I put everything else I'd found into the bags and stored them in my messenger bag. I'd stolen a few more long-sleeved t-shirts from the washing room, and hopefully, my own clothes would be dry by tomorrow, and I could bring them as well. I wouldn't get anywhere tonight, so I curled up on the sofa and tried to sleep.

It wasn't unusual for Myalgic Encephalomyelitis patients to have trouble sleeping, ironically, but yet again, I was so exhausted after the last few days that I slipped away without trouble.

The next morning I got up with my alarm, took my pills, and ate the last of the rice before bringing my bag to the bathroom. There, I washed my mouth and body as best I could with the limited resources I had left. I found that my clothes were dry and wrapped them in a big plastic bag to stuff into the messenger bag together with the rest of my catch. It was full to bursting and hard to handle, but I didn't dare leave any of it behind. Then I dressed and left the house.

It wasn't raining anymore, even if the sky was still grey. I hid beneath the cap I'd stolen from the house. It had the Linkin Park logo on it, so I guessed it had belonged to the teenager. I was as good as ready to go, but there was one more thing I wanted to do.

Taking the key I'd found in one of the kitchen drawers, I crawled on my improvised knee- and hand-pads to the double-garage. The big doors didn't have any handles, so I guessed they were electric, but the tag on the key said 'garage', so I crawled around until I found a door set on the side. Unlocking it, I clicked on my torch and took in the room.

There was a car on the far side, but without electricity, I couldn't get it out of the garage, which was a shame. I would have loved to drive to the station. I could drive but had stopped when I became a danger to myself and others because I couldn't concentrate on the road or what I was doing. Not like there were anyone else I could be a danger to these days.

Instead, I looked around for anything else that might help me get to the station faster. The beam glinted off matt metal, and I crawled closer, a grin spreading across my lips. A long-board stood against the wall, well kept and well used. Probably the kid's, but I didn't think he'd care if I borrowed it. If he and his family ever came back, I was sure they could afford a new one anyway.

With one hand rested on the long-board to guide it out the door, I turned to leave, but my eyes landed on a hoe standing up against the wall together with some other gardening tools. My smile broadened.

After two trips, I was ready to go. The street was still wet after the rain, but that wasn't a problem for the long-board as I sat on it, legs tucked underneath me, holding on to the hoe with both hands and using the butt end of it to push forward.

33

According to the map, there was a back-road that went almost all the way to the station without passing through any built-up areas or going close to the freeway. I hoped it was enough to keep me off any zombie-radars. Or living-radars for that matter.

I soon realized I'd miscalculated—not on the road to take, but on using a long-board to get where I needed to go. While the wheels were amazing on flat ground, this was Norway, and there was hardly any flat space to be found! To get out of the neighborhood and onto the side-road I wanted, I had to push myself up a small hill. Small for cars and bikes and people with working legs; not so small for someone pushing themselves along on a long-board.

By the time I reached the top, my arms were numb from exhaustion, and I was sweating despite the chill air.

I allowed myself to rest until my arms hurt from the work-out, then I continued. Thankfully, the road was at a slack downward hill from there, so I mostly had to use the hoe to break. The sound of the metal against asphalt made my teeth hurt, so I pushed in my earbuds when I stopped next time.

I didn't like not being able to hear well, but I trusted I would smell it if any zombies drew close, and I could only hope no one lived out here who might want to hurt me.

The next two hours were pretty much the same. Pushing up slack hills, resting, then rolling down the other side, hoping I wouldn't crash into anything. My control of the hoe and long-board had grown fine from the hands-on training, and I'd learned how to move the long-board around on the road, even park it while in the middle of a downward hill. I passed small groups of houses, all deserted, fields, and copses of trees. I didn't see anyone or anything, and the air was blessedly scent-free. Until it wasn't.

I was on my way down another slack hill when the first hint of rot hit my nose. I gagged, almost losing my grip on the hoe in surprise. Turning onto the shoulder of the road, I pulled up my bandana to cover my nose and plucked out my earbuds.

The sudden sound of the wind in the leaves of the bush beside me made me wince. It took me a moment to be able to hear anything else, but there wasn't much else to hear. The singing of birds somewhere far away, but no moaning or gurgling of the walking dead. No steps of living people following me either.

The wind blew in my face again, and I narrowed my eyes to see as far ahead as I could, but trees stood in the way, like a wall against the horizon.

I pulled out the map-book and flipped through it, trying to guess where I was. There was only one small town between Galleberg and me, and I hadn't passed that yet.

Putting the book in my pocket, I plugged in my earbuds again and pushed onto the road. To be safe, I turned the hoe around and used the butt end to steer with, so I had the sharp hoe as a weapon if needed. To avoid losing control, I pushed myself in a zig-zag down the street, keeping my speed down and giving myself more than enough time to look around.

Reaching the bottom of the hill, I kept to the middle of the road as I neared a line of trees. A sign came into view, telling me I was leaving Viken County and entering Vestfold og Telemark County, which was where the small town was.

I considered slowing down, give myself enough time to see everything there was to see, but I decided on getting through as fast as I could. I had a headache from the splintered light of the grey day and the sound of the hoe. My arms were tired and full of lactic acid. They were still working, but I feared they might stop if I slowed down. I knew that as long as I kept going, I would be OK. Tired and resistant, sure, but OK. It was when I stopped that things would get bad.

The trees passed by, and I came to a crossroads. After making sure there were no zombies around, despite the smell having grown stronger, I stopped and double-checked the map. When sure where I was going, I pushed forward.

The road turned downward into another lazy slope, and I let my speed build up, allowing myself to rest as much as I could. It wasn't so steep that I had to worry, and I could steer the long-board with my legs.

Leaning more weight on my right leg to follow the slow turn, bushes and trees changed to buildings ahead. The scent was strong here, and my eyes wanted to jump around and hunt for the source, but I didn't dare take my eyes off the road.

Ahead, another road fed into the one I was on, and something stepped from the opening. On instinct, I lowered my hoe to the ground. The sudden force of the connection dragged the hoe from my hands.

I screamed and leaned down on the long-board. Gripping the edges and using my body-weight, I was able to zoom past the person, who stumbled to reach me. Behind it, I saw more forms and knew I'd found the source of the smell.

And I'd just lost my weapon.

I wanted to look back–to see how far I was from the hoe, and how many zombies might be following me–but I didn't dare. The hill had gotten steeper, and I was gathering speed. Ahead, there was another turn, running through a small neighborhood. If someone stepped into the road, I wasn't sure I'd be able to avoid them.

Thankfully, the ground flattened out as I passed the first house. I still had a lot of speed, but it wasn't building anymore.

I managed to stay on the road as I flew through the neighborhood, and slowed enough to use one foot to help me turn onto the next street. The maneuver lost me a lot of speed and I soon slowed and stopped. Barely two houses away from the neighborhood and the zombies there.

For a moment, panic flooded through me. How would I keep moving without the hoe? It wasn't like I could stand on the long-board and push forward as intended. Remembering my original plan, I found the pieces of wood for my hands. Before fastening them, I took out my earbuds and stuffed them into my pocket, not bothering with their case. Right now, I just wanted to get as far away as possible.

Tucking my legs under me and out of the way, I leaned down and started dragging myself forward with my plank-covered hands. Soon, I'd built up enough momentum to leave the scent of the dead behind me.

Getting up and down the hills using my hands was a lot harder. I was constantly panting for breath, my shoulders and back ached, and my fingers were stiff and screaming from their grip on the planks. I didn't give myself time to stop, not even to take a painkiller. All that seemed to be left of my mind was pain and exhaustion. It kept The Fog at bay, but there wasn't much more going on.

I'm not sure I would have been able to take a painkiller. My hands had been gripping the hoe and the planks, and I'd been outside for so long and was so sweaty. Who knew how many germs were on my hands right now? Much less the rest of my body? Could I bring myself to put something I held with those hands into my mouth?

I'm not sure how long it was between the zombies and the first sign to Galleberg, but I think it was far enough to be safe. Only a small part of my brain recognized the name when I passed the sign, but it was enough for me to turn onto the small road. I passed a few houses, not even seeing them before I arrived at the last house on the street.

It was a small, one-story, white thing, with a bench out front and a sign on the wall claiming it was the same house as had once been Galleberg Togstasjon. There were no train-tracks in sight and no parking lot. As far as my tired mind could tell, the station had been shut down, and only the building was left. It had been turned into a public resting place, it seemed.

Tears leaked from my eyes and stung my sweaty cheeks, but I was too tired to cry properly.

Using the same instinct that had gotten me here alive, I made my way to the building and crawled onto the porch. The door was unlocked, and I crawled inside, not even looking around before I closed and locked the door behind me. I noticed it smelled of old paper and dust, then I curled up on the floor and passed out.

The next time I woke, I was able to take in the interior of the building. It was only one room, with a fireplace in one corner and a heap of wood beside it. There were a couch and a few blankets, a table and a small kitchenette. When looking through the cabinets, I saw that they held a few bags of instant-soup and cocoa, as well as some tea. There was a door leading to a bathroom, where I cleaned up as best I could and changed into clean clothes.

Afterwards, I made myself a nest on the floor beside the sofa, as far from the door as I could get. I used the pillows from the sofa and the blanket, as well as what softness I had brought myself. It wasn't much, but it felt safer. I fell asleep there, partly hidden.

When I woke up again, I was able to push the sofa, so it shielded me completely from the door, and any visitors would have to crawl over it to get at me.

Over the next few days, I moved the sofa enough, so the only way in was through a small opening on my side. It was cold, and I was sick. A fever ran through my body and gave me nightmares. I used the wood to light a fire at night, not caring if anyone saw the smoke.

I forced myself to eat and drink, always boiling the water twice before risking it. André had said boiling water killed the worms, right? I couldn't remember, could only hope.

The days ran together until they were a mess of feeling awful and surviving. When the fever finally let go, I continued keeping the fire going at night, for it was chilly, and I felt weaker than I had in a long time.

My mind kept wandering, wondering what I should do next. Should I stay here and hope Shadia found me? Even if it wasn't a proper train station? Or should I try to get to the next station when I felt stronger? How many days had it been since Drammen? How long would Shadia wait? Forever. I knew that because I would wait forever for her. But what if we waited for each other in the wrong place? And I would soon be out of both food and medical supplies. There were a few houses close by I could raid, but nothing else. I was in the middle of no-where and on my own. That thought broke what little willpower I had left.

34

It was still early on my seventh day at Galleberg, but I was awake, lying in my nest and trying to keep warm, to find a reason to care. The last embers of my fire were dying, leaving the scent of burned wood and ash in the air.

The door rattled. I couldn't see it from where I was hiding, but I could clearly hear the lock against the frame as someone tried to force it open.

Carefully, I reached for my knife. I'd created my nest with this in mind. If they got inside, they wouldn't see me unless they knew where to look. If I was lucky, they wouldn't notice me at all and just leave when they got what they came for. If I was unlucky, I would have to fight. I really didn't want that. My joints were swollen and clumsy from the cold. I wasn't sure I could put up a fight even if I wanted to.

The door rattled again before something slammed into it: the thwack of an ax.

A gust of cold, wet air snuck through the opening of my nest and started kissing whatever skin it could reach. I shivered before moving as quietly as I could into the darkest corner of my little cave, making sure to pull the blankets with me to stay warm.

The door opened, and I heard boots on the concrete floor,

followed by the door closing again.

"Kit?" I blinked against sudden tears. *"Habibi?* Are you here?"

"Shadia," I whispered, my voice low and rough from the cold and lack of use. I'd stopped talking to myself on day two. Clearing my throat, I tried again. "Sha!"

She drew a deep, shaking breath before I heard her move again.

After another silence, I crawled around the corner.

Shadia stood with one hand on the counter by her side. She looked tired. Her hair was almost flat from natural oils, and she had big bags under her eyes. Her cheekbones looked a lot sharper than they had the last time I saw her, and her yoga pants looked a little loose. There was blood on her arms and legs, but it was all dark and half-dried.

"Sha," I breathed, then she was on the ground with me, wrapping her arms around me and pulling me close.

I grabbed the back of her jacket and tried to bury myself in her chest. She smelled pretty bad, but I didn't care, for it was her own scent; the scent of jasmine and heat and Shadia. She drew a deep breath before pulling away from me a little. Her hands stroked my hair, my face, my shoulders, as her eyes roamed over me, looking for I didn't know what. Then she kissed me. It wasn't a hungry kiss, but it was urgent. I kissed her back, trying to bury myself in her and be as close to her as I possibly could be. Water touched my lips, and I drew back. Shadia shuddered in my arms before she started sobbing. I sniffed, wiping my own tears before I pulled her to me, hugging her.

"It's OK," I whispered into her hair. "It's OK." She shuddered again, gasping for breath as she tried to talk through her tears.

"Not yet. You can tell me later." She nodded and grabbed me, hiding her face between my breasts before she howled.

She cried for a long time, but her howls died down fast enough, replaced by the quiet, helpless sobs that no human can control.

I kissed her behind the ear, my own silent tears falling.

"How long have you been here?" she asked, pushing away to look at me.

I counted in my head. "Seven nights."

"That long?"

"Yeah."

I could see she wanted to say something more, but I kissed her. It was a fast peck, for I was afraid I'd drown in her if I kissed her any more, and pulled her toward my nest.

Inside, I motioned for Shadia to sit on the blankets while I found a packet of wet napkins. When I turned, Shadia was sitting where I'd told her, looking around the small room I'd made myself.

"Here," I said and handed her the napkins. "Clean yourself up." The motion of doing something familiar calmed my shaking hands.

Shadia accepted the napkins but just stared at them for a while. She drew another shuddering breath and looked at me. "I'm so sorry it took so long." I looked at her. "For taking so long."

"Sha ..." I began, but she shook her head.

"I thought you were dead."

I crawled to her and took her face in my hands, forcing her to look at me when she opened her eyes again. "But I'm not. I'm right here, and I'm fine. And now you're here, and we can finally get going."

Her lips were trembling, but she nodded and pulled me into another hug. I stayed there, sitting on my knees, her face between my breasts, murmuring nonsense until she calmed down again. When I pulled away, she was trying to hide a big yawn.

"But for now," I said, using my business voice, "you should clean yourself up."

"I'm fine," she mumbled around the yawn.

"M-hm," I answered, crossing my arms and looking down at her.

"You don't believe me?" she asked, a glint in her eyes.

"Not at all."

"Then you know how I feel all the time."

I rolled my eyes. "Yeah, yeah, I'm a poor patient. Now, get cleaned up!"

She smiled, even if it didn't reach her eyes.

After washing my own hands in antibacterial gel, I helped her get out of her bloody clothes and clean her body. She smelled stale and of anxiety, but still of herself. Always of herself.

While cleaning, she told me that she got off the bridge in a kind of trance, just thinking that she had to find me, had to find me, had to find me. She searched the shore for two days but didn't even see a footprint. We agreed that I must have washed up further down. How she made her way to Sanden Stasjon, the next train station, and waited. Then she found a car and drove to the next station, hoping I may have missed Sanden, even if she knew it was too far for me to go. When I hadn't arrived by her fourth day there, she started wandering up and down the back roads. That was how she smelled my smoke, and now here she was.

When we were done cleaning her, she helped do the same to my hands and my face.

She cried four times while telling the story, but none as bad as that first round. I don't think her body was able to cry any harder at the moment, exhausted as it was. I cried with her. She was here! She was finally here!

"I missed you so much," I managed.

"I missed you too, *habibi*. I'm sorry I took so long," she murmured and kissed the top of my head.

I wanted to say that she should stop saying sorry, but couldn't find the words, so I just gave myself over to tears. When I calmed down, the adrenaline of finally seeing Shadia again was slipping away. She noticed and forced me to drink cola from her own bag before she found both our sleeping bags. She only had one rucksack, but she promised the rest of our stuff was in her new car. Apart from my wheelchair. She hadn't been able to bring it when escaping the zombies.

I didn't care. We could find a new one.

I wanted to help her set up the sleeping bags, but my hands were shaking again, so she pushed me away, trying to make jokes about it. I tried to laugh, but we were both too aware of having almost lost each other.

Finally, she zipped the two sleeping bags together, and we undressed and crawled into them, holding on to each other as if we would never let go again.

35

Shadia's hands roamed my body. One found my breast, taking hold and massaging. The other moved up and down my skin, leaving trails of fire. I was still wearing my jeans, but one of her thighs was pressed between my legs, and I rubbed against it, moaning, begging her with my eyes to come closer, to undress.

"Not yet," she said, smiling down at me.

Her trailing hand moved up, stroked over my throat, and tilted my head backwards. Her fingers were at my lips, and I parted them, ready to take her into me there if nowhere else, but her hands stopped moving, and her body grew stiff.

"Sha?" I said, opening my eyes to look at her. Her eyes were on something just below my face.

"What is that?" she asked, moving her hand from my lips to touch something on my throat, just below my jaw. At her touch, a sting of pain lanced down my throat, and I winced. "Habibi?"

"I don't know," I said, moving away from her and standing.

With her hot on my heels, I walked into the bathroom and looked in the mirror. Leaning over the sink and tilting my head back, I looked at the bump that had formed on my throat. Poking it, another sting of pain radiated outward.

"What is it?" Shadia asked, standing in the doorway, hugging

226

herself.

"Dunno," I answered and pulled back. "But it's probably fine. It'll be gone in a day or two, I'm sure."

"You aren't going to the doctor?"

"Why bother? It's just a swollen something or other."

I took her in my arms and kissed her neck, trying to find my way back to where we had just been, but Shadia pushed me away.

"Don't. You had that fever last week, and you've been feeling weird. You're going to the doctor."

"It's just the season," I argued, trying to grab her again, but she stepped back.

"If you don't call the doctor, I will, and I will drag you there by your hair if I have to."

"Fine! I'll do it. But I swear, I've just had the flu, and this is just a swollen tonsil. You'll feel stupid when they tell me it's nothing."

Shadia walked into the bedroom and found my phone. "Then I'll feel stupid, but better safe than sorry." She held the phone out to me.

"You worry too much," I mumbled as I looked up the number online.

"You don't worry enough," she answered, kissing me on the cheek and leaning against my shoulder as I put the phone to my ear.

I woke to Shadia trailing her fingers along my naked shoulder, across my back, and over my hips. Letting out a satisfied sound, I turned and looked at her. She was propped up on one elbow, her head resting on her hand, as her other hand rested on my stomach.

I almost couldn't believe she was here with me; that we found each other again. That we were alive.

"How're you feeling?" I asked before she had the chance.

She was looking a little better. The bags under her eyes were smaller, and her cheeks looked a little less hollow.

"Still tired, but OK. Everything is OK now." She tickled my stomach, and I grimaced.

Her smile widened, and she started tickling me again, aiming for those spots she knew would make me laugh. I grabbed for her hand, trying to keep it away from those spots even as she poked at them. I gurgled a laugh before I pushed the arm away. She fought my grip, pulling me closer until she almost fell over me. We tussled until she lay on her back with my head on her shoulder, one arm under me and one partly over me, hand resting on my hip again. It felt good to be close to her. To just be us for a while.

"So, what's the plan?" I asked after our breathing was back under control, and I started feeling sleepy again.

"We should get moving, but it depends on what you can handle," Shadia answered.

When I looked up at her, I saw she had her eyes closed, so I did the same.

"If you're sure, we should consider getting a move on. Spend the night here, then go tomorrow?"

I played with a strand of her hair, brushing it along her breastbone and collarbones. Even without eyes, I knew her body better than I knew my own. "You have a car?" I asked, remembering her story.

"Yes, but it's not here. I left it at the station, not wanting to waste gas."

"Then how will we get me anywhere? I don't think I can crawl any length of time without adrenalin and a pack of angry men chasing me."

Shadia scoffed. "I can look around tomorrow. Some of the

houses around here must have something."

We lay for a long while, her hand moving slower and slower across my back as drowsiness claimed us. Her hand stopped moving, and she hugged me a little tighter, turning her body to lie more comfortably, and her hand moved down my stomach and stopped just at the edge of my underwear.

"How are you feeling?" she whispered into my ear.

I turned in her arms, resting one hand on her hip and pushing the other under her, letting my fingers rest in her hair. "I'm feeling fine."

"You sure?"

I kissed her in answer, and she kissed me back. I could feel her worry melt away as she pulled me as close as she could—so close I wasn't sure where I stopped, and she began. Then we made love.

* * *

"You think anyone heard us?" Shadia said afterwards, lying on her side, her forehead touching mine, our hands folded together between our breasts.

"You're loud, so if anyone's around, they'd have heard," I said around a yawn.

"I'm not that loud!"

"Yes, you are." I grinned. "I know just what to do to make you scream."

She furrowed her brow. "What? Torture? I guess that's a fitting word."

"Hey!"

"I'm just kidding, *habibi*." She kissed my nose before turning around and cuddling her back against my front. "But we should sleep now."

"That's my line," I mumbled around another yawn.

"Not anymore. Sleep."

"I thought I was the bossy one."

She chuckled but didn't say anything, and neither did I.

In the end, I did fall asleep and only woke when my clock told me it was time to take my medication.

Sitting up, I looked around. Shadia was nowhere to be seen, and her clothes and ax were both gone.

"Sha?" I asked, keeping my voice low just in case I wasn't alone. She had to be here somewhere, right? Her finding me hadn't been a dream. It couldn't be a dream.

"Shadia?" I tried again, raising my voice a little.

The door opened, and boots walked across the concrete floor, drawing ever closer. It was Shadia. It had to be Shadia. Didn't it?

"Kit? You awake?"

I let out my held breath as she poked her head into the nest. "Where were you?" I asked, aware that my voice was hard.

Shadia blinked at me. "I checked out a few of the closer houses. Like we talked about."

"We talked about checking it out together," I snapped.

Shadia's whole face softened. "*Habibi*, what is this really about?"

"Don't disappear on me like that, OK?"

"OK. I'm sorry." She crawled over and hugged me to her, kissing away the one tear that escaped from my eyes.

I sniffed, blinking away tears. "You'd better be."

She chuckled and squeezed before sitting back on her haunches. "Have you taken your meds?"

"Not yet."

Giving me a mock-frown, she started looking around until she found my medication and a can of cola to get it down.

"Did you find anything?" I asked before putting the pills in my mouth.

She smiled. "A wheelbarrow."

My eyebrows shot up. "A wheelbarrow?"

"Yes." Her smile died, and she looked away. "I thought maybe you could sit in it, and I could push you until we find a better solution."

I looked at her for a long time before I started laughing.

"What?" She asked. "It's a good idea."

"It is, it is." I snorted. "The mental picture was just really weird, is all."

Pursing her lips to keep from laughing herself, Shadia swatted my arm. The look on her face made me laugh harder, and with a mumbled 'why, you' Shadia clambered over me and started tickling me again, yelling that she would give me something to laugh about. Between screaming in laughter and begging her to stop, I managed to wrap my arms around her and turn us around until she was beneath me. Pinning her arms across her chest, using my whole weight to keep them there, I kissed her nose and all over her face until I could control my laughter again. When I pulled back, Shadia was grinning from ear to ear. Her arms free, she reached up and pulled me down again, kissing me over both eyes, on my nose, on both cheekbones, my lips.

"How tired are you?" she asked in-between kisses.

"Not at all," I answered the next time she moved to kiss another part of my face.

Her lips trailed from my jaw and to the base of my throat. "Are you sure?"

I bit my lower lip to keep from gasping. "Yes."

Her hands slid from my shoulders and down my naked back, leaving trails of fire until they rested on my hips. She moved her own hips beneath me, lifting a leg to push against my groin. I let the gasp out this time before looking down at her face. It wore a wicked smile, and her eyes were warm and narrow as she looked at me. I drowned in those eyes and let her flip me before we drowned in each other.

Excerpt from Medical Notebook

Unlike in most TV shows, books, and comics, these zombies were controlled by nature. Meaning they would decompose as normal bodies, if a little slower. The more fresh meat they ate, the longer the body was held together, but even the best hunters would eventually rot away their muscles, unable to move, leaving the worm to starve, and finally letting the dead rest in peace.

36

I slept fitfully that night, constantly dreaming of Shadia disappearing. When I woke, whimpering, she was right there, shushing me and holding me. Finally, I slipped into an exhausted sleep after the day's events and dreamed no more.

The next morning, we ate a quick breakfast before Shadia cleaned up my nest. I sat and watched, not allowed to help. That was OK. I'd stopped, after all, and as I feared, getting my body going again was hard. Shadia brought our bags outside before she came in to get me.

I hadn't been outside since arriving at the old train station, and what greeted me gave me a start. There were bodies everywhere, all dead and ... melting.

"Where did they come from?" I asked as Shadia tried not to step on any of them.

"They were here when I arrived," she answered.

"But ... why didn't I hear them? And why do they look like that?"

"Like what?"

"All melted."

"They're decomposing."

"This fast?"

"I think the rain may have had something to do with it. And you didn't hear them because they were too weak to do anything. When I came, most of them were just leaning against the wall. They hardly even turned when I killed them. I blame the fire you had going inside. It was warmer than me."

"Warmer?"

"Yes. I think they can sense heat, like a snake. That is why they were drawn to the fire instead of us, and why they were drawn to André when we stood side by side. He had a fever, so he was the warmest of us." She stopped at the other end of the street, away from the bodies.

"That makes sense," I mumbled, thinking about every encounter we'd had. How the zombies seemed to see us even when we were inside a building and away from the windows. The wheelbarrow Shadia had found was wide and covered in blankets that looked rough but would cushion my butt over the metal.

After a little back and forth, Shadia was able to lower me into it. It was just as hard as I'd thought, despite the blankets, and smelled of hay and kibble. There was no sign of the source of the scents, so I was pretty sure it was the blankets. Someone living around here must have had bunnies or something, and a hoard of them, if they needed a wheelbarrow to feed them. I wondered what had happened to the animals now, but decided not to ask. Hopefully, they'd gotten out and were free somewhere. More likely, zombies had broken into their cage and eaten them.

Shadia arranged the blankets and bags around me so I wouldn't be thrown around too much as we moved, and I took comfort in her closeness as I tried to forget about the bunnies. I was suddenly really glad the apocalypse had forced us to become vegetarian.

"Ready?" Shadia asked as she repositioned one of the bags so I could get to her ax easier.

"As ready as I'll ever be," I answered and huddled into the fabric around me.

Shadia bent and kissed the tip of my nose, pulled up my bandana to cover it, and walked out of sight.

The wheelbarrow jerked, and I gripped the ax hard as I swayed off the ground. It felt like I was on a boat, waves hitting against the sides, as Shadia found the balancing point before she backed up and turned, wheeling me down the slope toward the road.

The rest of the day was mostly uneventful. We met two zombies that Shadia took out long before they became a danger to us. The encounters made it clear we had to find another ax, as Shadia didn't want to leave me without one, and I didn't want her to get any closer to the zombies than she had to, which happened when she used the knife to give them mercy. She didn't disagree with me, but wouldn't go searching for one either. If she stumbled over one, however, she would take it.

"Promise?" I asked.

"Yes."

I heard a smile in her voice and wondered why, but didn't ask. Instead, I leaned my head back, squinting to keep the weak sun out of my eyes, and looked up at her. "Pinkie promise?" I lifted my hand, all fingers but the pinkie curled into a fist.

Shadia sighed and rolled her eyes, but wrapped one of her pinkies around mine. "I swear."

I would have answered 'good' and told her I loved her, but the wheelbarrow started tipping when she let go with one hand, and I was too busy not falling out or dumping all our stuff on the ground to speak.

We moved past houses and homes, fields, and forests. Now and again, we saw the edge of a town or settlement not far away, but we never got near them. We ate on the go, not wanting to spend any more time in the open than we had to, and before dinner, Shadia said we were close.

I sat up straighter, having been napping in the barrow, nursing my stomach, that was feeling seasick from the motion and the uneven ground.

In front were houses, and past them even more houses, but all seemed quiet.

"Were there many zombies here?" I asked, not taking my eyes off the road.

Shadia only made a 'hmm'-sound that could mean both yes and no.

We passed the first houses and came to an open area with football fields and playgrounds. There were tents and chain link fences set up, but no sign of people, living or dead. A church came into view, and I saw that the front doors were covered in a rust-like color. I'd come to associate it with dried blood, but again there were no bodies.

There were no bodies until we entered the town proper, where the road was splattered with the remains of them. It looked like someone had driven over them again and again, not stopping until there was nothing but mush left.

My stomach heaved, but I was able to keep my small lunch down as I turned and looked up at Shadia. She didn't look down, just stared right ahead, her jaw set end eyes hard.

"I'm glad I'm not on your bad side," I said, and she snorted, her eyes softening and jaw loosening as she glanced down at me. "I mean, look at this. You went full Mad Max on their poor asses!"

She snorted another laugh, and I smiled as I turned back around.

Ahead, I could see a sign pointing to the station, but my eyes were drawn to a set of open doors. Beside them stood a sign saying 'library'. There was no blood and no bodies.

I turned again. "Wait, did you take time to go to the library?"

This time, Shadia actually laughed. When she stopped, she jostled the wheelbarrow to turn me forward again. I narrowed my eyes at her.

"It was boring just waiting for you," she finally answered.

I chuckled and turned forward again. Leave it to Shadia to break into a library during the apocalypse.

There wasn't really a proper train station waiting for us as I had expected. Shadia rolled me past the big parking lot. It was splattered with blood and body parts, and it looked like she'd been just driven around and around, killing anything that followed her.

Instead of the train station, she took me to the fire station, which made me smile. No wonder she knew where there might be more fire axes. There was a lot of blood here as well, but she rolled me past it and around to the back, where she parked by a door.

Without a word, she lifted me from the barrow and carried me to the door, using a key to open it, and carried me inside like I was a bride on my wedding night. I considered making a joke but was too tired, the sight of the library and the blood having taken the last of my energy.

Shadia seemed just as exhausted as she only carried me up three sets of stairs and into a room filled with single beds. She lowered me onto one of them, and I smelled her jasmine scent on the pillow.

"I'll get our stuff. You rest," she said and kissed my temple.

I smiled at her as she stood and left the room before I closed my eyes.

I didn't sleep, but I may have dozed as Shadia moved around downstairs. I heard her lock doors and start a car. Finally, she came upstairs again and dragged one of the other beds over to stand beside me. She'd brought food, and we ate in bed before we lay down, holding each other.

I was deep in my own thoughts when she spoke. "How did you get there?"

"Hm?"

"How did you get to the old station? You never told me."

I drew in a deep breath and held it for a moment before I told her about the trip down-river, about the boat, the planks and crawling, the house, the long-board, and finally the old station. It wasn't a long story, and it almost felt a little anti-climactic compared to Shadia running around looking for me. I'd spent two weeks getting from the river and to the station. It wasn't even far inland. That said, I had to take my health into consideration. I was both proud and felt like a failure by the time I was done speaking.

Shadia lay quiet for a time before she pushed up on one elbow and looked down at me. She stroked a faded green lock of hair away from my face. I'd been chewing on it while waiting for her to speak. Was I that addicted to chewing gum? I'd eat my own hair if I didn't get any?

"I am so sorry," Shadia said, her brown eyes meeting mine and holding them. "I am so sorry; I couldn't save you."

"Hey!" I reached up with one hand and rested it against her

cheek. My skin looked pale, almost blue, against her warm tones. "What'd I say about saying sorry?"

She smiled, but it didn't quite reach her eyes. Instead of answering, she lay on top of me, wrapping both arms around me and squeezing. "I am never letting you go again!"

I laughed and mock-fought to get away. Even as we laughed and joked, I could feel the fear in her. The fear that she'd almost lost me. The fact that she was blaming herself. The fear of what those two weeks would do to my health.

With Myalgic Encephalomyelitis, everything you did came with a price. How high would that price be for me? And when would I have to pay it? Today? Tomorrow? In a month? Whenever the crash came, it would come hard, I didn't doubt that for a second, and hoped the constant reminder of us not being safe would be enough to get us to the cabin. Would hold it off until we actually were safe.

I didn't sleep much that night, just dozed on and off. It was a relief when my alarm woke us at nine in the morning.

We ate breakfast in bed and cleaned up in the bathroom before Shadia carried me downstairs again and into the garage. There were two firetrucks there, gleaming red and white in the light coming through the frosted windows. I couldn't help staring. I'd never actually seen a firetruck up close before.

"Why can't we take one of them?" I asked as Shadia walked to a dirty SUV standing between the cars.

"I don't know how to drive them," she answered and opened the passenger door.

"I do!"

"No, you don't."

"Aw, come on! It would be awesome." She gave me a look as she helped me into the seat, and I rolled my eyes. "Fine. Not

240

like we're into driving firetruck anyway."

She cocked her head and opened her mouth to ask what I meant, but the grin on my face must have given it away. "Kit, that's nasty."

"I said we weren't into it!"

She slammed the door and stuck her tongue out at me. I waggled my own at her, and she laughed as she headed toward the stairs again.

One more trip and all our stuff was in the car.

"Speaking of firetrucks, have you had your period yet?" she asked, moving things around in the back of the car.

"No," I answered, looking away. "It's not like I've been able to eat any more over the last month."

She didn't answer, but I could feel her worry across the length of the car. I'd stopped having my period two months before the first zombie case. I didn't eat much, and stopping the menstruation cycle was a natural part of starvation, but it wasn't a healthy thing, so it worried everyone who cared about me. It worried me as well.

Without a word, Shadia closed the door with a slam that made me jump. She gave me an apologetic smile as she slid into the seat beside me and started the car. Squeezing my thigh, she stepped out again, leaving the car door open. The garage doors were electric, but there was a pulley system on one side, and she used that to drag it open.

I sat forward in my seat, afraid there might be undead waiting on the other side, but there was nothing. Not even a bird to stare at us in wonder.

When the door opened enough to let us drive under, Shadia jogged back and crawled into the seat.

"Seatbelt," she said.

I pulled at it to indicate I was ready, and she closed her door and revved the engine. We left the town of Sande behind, never looking back.

37

Being back in a car was both weird and calming all at once. It felt like things were normal. Like we were just going to a doctor's appointment or to some friends, or even the movies. Before I got too sick to hang out with our friends or go to the movies, anyway. But in-between that feeling of normalcy was the constant fact that things weren't normal. That when Shadia made a sharp turn, it was to avoid a car left in the road, blood on its windows, or the crawling torso of some unlucky soul. Shadia actually drove over the torso, making sure to crush the skull in the process. It was the merciful thing to do, we agreed.

I dozed a little, and we talked about this and that. About what we would do when we got to the cabin. We hadn't brought the wheelbarrow or a new wheelchair, so we knew we had to find something that would make it easier for me to move around. Then again, maybe I wouldn't need it? Maybe all of this had been the cure I needed? It was OK to hope, right?

We were almost at the old border between Vestfold and Telemark, and Shadia was mumbling about us having to find some more gas. She had, apparently, not thought about stealing gas from any of the other cars in Sande, and I couldn't blame her. I hadn't thought of it either, and I was the one who was supposed to have watched a bunch of zombie shows.

I had the map open in my lap, looking for the easiest way to get to a town. There was apparently a small hamlet not far from here, and we had to drive past it anyway to get to the freeway. While we'd avoided it so far, we had to get onto it now, as it was the fastest way to the cabin. The alternative was driving farther inland and possibly lengthening the trip by two hours. Now that we were so close, we didn't want to put it off any longer. We were almost safe.

"Whalla," Shadia said, but I wasn't sure if it was a curse or surprise, and I barely had time to look up before she stepped on the brakes and we skidded to a halt.

I was about to ask what was up when I saw it.

We were on the top of a hill, the road leading into a small dump before going up another hill. There were trees all around, and we had been driving alone for a long time. Now, as I watched, another car stopped halfway down the hill opposite us. It was a blue truck, looking well used. Nothing like the black cars of Nicholas and his men. Still, that's where my mind went.

"You think it's them?" Shadia asked, taking the words out of my mouth.

"Nicholas?" I asked, just to be sure, and she nodded. "No," I continued, tasting the word. "I don't think they'd drive a car like that. He was too proud."

Shadia snorted, but there was no humor in it. "So, who are they?"

I shook my head, unable to answer.

The car in front of us blinked its lights and started rolling down the hill. It didn't pick up much speed and stopped when it was on the small, flat area at the bottom of the little valley between us. Both front doors opened, and two men stepped out. One was older, his hair completely white, and his skin dark from hours spent in the sun. The other man didn't seem much older than us, in his late thirties, maybe.

"What do we do?" I asked.

Shadia turned and looked at me. "They might be able to help us. Give us gas and such?"

"If they let us go again," I answered.

We stared at each other for a long moment before Shadia sighed. "I'm taking the chance. We need the help."

I grabbed her hand, and she turned to look at me again. "Be careful," I said, hoping she could see all the feelings welling in my eyes, despite my sunglasses.

Nodding, she pulled her hand free and started the car again. It rolled a little, but instead of driving to the bottom of the hill, she turned it onto the shoulder of the road, my door leading into the brush.

"If it seems like I'm in trouble, get out and get away," she said.

"Shadia," I growled.

She spoke over me. "And if it seems OK, stay in the car until I wave at you, OK? They don't look like Nicholas and his men, but who knows what they will say and think about someone in a wheelchair?"

I looked at the two men and their working clothes. "They may not be happy to help someone who can't help them in return," I said.

Shadia's jaw tightened, but she nodded.

"But maybe they have a spare wheelchair we can take," I said, trying to sound happy and unworried.

Shadia turned to me and took my hand. She kissed it before

she unbuckled her seatbelt and crawled out, shutting the door behind her.

Unhurried, she walked onto the road and headed down the hill.

I watched her go before I crawled into her seat. She'd turned off the car, but I sat ready to start it if needed. I would not leave Shadia behind, not if there was any chance of us getting away. Wasn't like I could get far in the forest anyway. Might as well take the chance, right? I couldn't help but smile, almost wanting the men to do something stupid so I could barrel down on them.

Shadia reached the men, and they started talking. I couldn't hear them from up here and inside the car and mumbled a curse that I hadn't rolled the windows down or something before Shadia left. I noticed that no one shook each other's hands, and I wondered if it was an insult toward Shadia, or just everyone being careful.

After what felt like forever, Shadia turned and waved at me.

For half a second, I considered driving down the road but decided to follow Shadia's orders instead. I opened the door, made sure my Linkin Park cap was in place, and stepped out, leaning on the door so I wouldn't put too much weight on my legs.

"Hey," I said, waving down at them.

Shadia said something too low for me to hear, and they all started walking toward me.

"Why can't she come to us?" the younger man asked, his voice booming up the hill.

"She can't walk," Shadia said.

"What d'you mean? She's standing right there."

"She uses a wheelchair to get around, and we lost it a while back."

The younger man stopped, gaping up at me. The older man noticed and slapped him on the shoulder. "Manners," he growled.

The younger closed his mouth before clearing his throat and hurrying to catch up with Shadia again. "I'm sorry," he said. "I just ... I didn't know anyone like ... that ... still lived. I'm sorry. I'm being rude. I don't mean to, I just ..." he babbled himself into silence.

"Can't blame you," I said, shrugging.

The young man blushed on realizing I'd heard him and looked down at his feet.

"So you two need help getting 'cross the lake?" the older man asked.

"Any help at all would be welcome," Shadia answered.

"Where'd you travel from?"

"Oslo," Shadia answered. Her voice sounded as tired as I felt.

The old one whistled in what sounded like awe. They walked in silence until they reached us. "I'm Martin, this fool is my brother-in-law, Christian. Who are you?"

"I'm Shadia." She nodded toward me. "And this is my wife, Kit."

Martin seemed to jump a little at that but kept his face empty of any feelings. Christian looked between us but didn't say anything. Neither of the men seemed angry or hateful, just curious as if they had never actually seen lesbians before.

"We'll give you a ride to town, and you can get cleaned up and have a good meal and some sleep," Martin said. "Tomorrow, we'll talk about how to get you 'cross the lake."

"Why do you keep talking about a lake?" I asked.

"The roads're over-run," Martin said. "Not just cars, but

the dead, both walking and not. We tried raiding Larvik last week and almost lost four men 'fore we were even 'cross the highway. Not going back that way, for sure. The only way 'cross now's by boat, or go further North."

"Oh," I said, glancing up at Shadia. Her face was drawn, and she was chewing on her bottom lip, thinking.

"Don't worry; we'll figure something out. Unless you wanna stay, 'course."

There was nothing in his voice to set me on edge, but I could still feel adrenalin spike through my body at those words. I looked at Shadia, but she was staring into the distance.

"It's a pretty good place, all things considered," Christian said, probably noticing my hesitation. "We're just a small hamlet, really, but we've got our own deep-water well, so we didn't get contaminated when SHTF."

"SHTF?" Shadia asked.

"Shit hit the fan," both Christian and I answered at once, and he grinned.

Still smiling, he continued. "Anyway, we got clear. Managed to snag a bunch of farm animals, have enough fields to keep us fed for a good while. We've built fences and gotten a hold of as many weapons as we can. We've raided everywhere we can get to, so we have a lot of everything. As far as we've seen, we're the only place still standing like this, and we've taken in a few others lucky enough to escape the worst of it. You know, we actually have a guy that got sick but survived?"

Christian continued to talk, but I tuned him out as Shadia looked at me.

"What do you think?" she said in a low voice. Christian continued speaking as if not hearing her.

"I think it's as good a deal as any. Especially considering

we're almost out of gas," I answered just as low. "And at least we'll be on guard. We'll know if something feels wrong. And it doesn't so far," I added the last as an afterthought, but Shadia was nodding, clearly agreeing with me.

"You can drive your own car," Martin said. He'd followed our conversation without a word. "So you've a way out if you wanna." His eyes glinted with a smile, even if his lips stayed still.

"Actually, we're almost out of gas," Shadia answered truthfully.

"Then you're welcome to ride 'long with us. You mind if we take what gas you've got left?"

Shadia shook her head.

After a short discussion, Christian was sent down to get their car, and Martin started emptying our car of stuff. He asked a few questions about my condition as I sat in the front seat, waiting. Shadia answered for me, and when she mentioned the cancer treatment that started it all, he only nodded once. He didn't say much after that, not until Christian had emptied our gas tank, and we were as ready to go as we would be.

"I've a chair left from my wife's, so you can take that if you wanna."

I thanked him, but couldn't miss the shocked look on Christian's face. It made me wonder about these men and their families, their lives, and I was actually looking forward to getting to find out more.

38

"So, what's the story of this village of yours?" Shadia asked.

She was sitting in one of the window seats as I lay stretched over the two other seats, head in her lap. Christian had taken the driver's seat and was taking it slow, after a request from Shadia, so I could relax. He kept glancing at us in the rear-view mirror, as if to check we were really there.

Martin answered her question. "'Tis not really a village as you'd expect. More like a few houses on a hill that share the same water source."

"Which is an underground well that hasn't been contaminated?" Shadia continued.

"Yeah," Christian answered.

Martin made a huffing sound before he continued. "Correct. It includes a few farms with their own water source spread across the valley, but they're usually just two or three houses at the most, and we've realized that we can't protect 'em all. Some stubborn fools stayed in their homes 'course, but the rest of us have worked together to set up a fence around the farms and the houses on the hill. Still not done, but we've got a lot of land secured."

I'd closed my eyes and almost drifted off to the deep drone of his voice, but Shadia moved beneath me, and I sat up straight, grabbing for my new ax where it lay on the floor. Before I could do anything, Shadia shushed me and pulled my head back down into her lap again. When I looked up at her, I saw she'd been rooting around in her rucksack and pulled out André's notebook.

"According to someone we traveled with," she said as she flipped through the book. "There was a chance the blood of the zombies could be a problem. If it was spilled on fertile ground later used to grow crops? Have you taken any precautions against that?"

I glanced toward the front in time to see Christian turn to look at us, then realize he should keep his eyes on the road and turning forward instead.

"We haven't really got any walkers up this far," Martin said. "There was a big fire in Larvik a few weeks ago, and it drew 'em like moths to a flame, pardon my cliché."

Silence fell over the car, and I drifted into an uneasy sleep. I'd never liked sleeping in the car, and that was no different now, but I was too tired to keep my eyes open. I woke once as the men and Shadia were talking about something, but I drifted away before I could hang on to whatever it was. When I woke next, it was from Shadia shaking me.

"Kit," she mumbled. "Wake up. You've got to see this."

I forced my eyes open and found she had removed my sunglasses and draped something over my face. I fumbled around before feeling the glasses pressed into my hand. Pushing them on and removing the fabric, I sat up and looked out and saw only trees. The road under the car was uneven and bumpy, and looking through the front window, I saw it was just a dirt road. On either side of us were trees rising up high, with huge, moss-filled stones in-between.

When I glanced at Shadia in confusion–I'd been seeing trees for the last few days now, after all–she pointed up at the window in the ceiling. Leaning against her and looking up and out, I finally saw what had caught her attention.

Mountains. Mountains rose on either side of us, tall and stark. The road was winding its way deeper in between the mountains, which must have worked as a natural wall to keep the zombies from even noticing the people living there.

A few minutes later, Christian slowed down as we neared an open area. It looked like the clearing had been thick woods until recently, for the ground was littered with stumps, freshly cut. The ground even had some sawdust spread around. Some two-hundred meters from the edge of the forest, a wall rose out of nothing. It was built of freshly cut timber and reached some three meters into the air. The only somewhat low part was what I guessed was a gate, and it was pulled to the side as we drew near.

Christian drove us through the gateway and stopped. The wooden gate rolled closed behind us, caging us between it and a chicken-wire fence running three meters high on either side of us.

On the other side of the wire, were people holding hunting rifles. Actual shooting weapons. They were both scary and a relief. I'd never seen a gun in real life, but in every zombie show I'd seen, guns were easily found. That wasn't the case here in Norway. The part of me that kept comparing my life to a zombie-show felt somewhat safer at the sight of those guns, but the part of me that was raised to think of guns as something dangerous and limited, something that killed, wanted to hide within the car.

Instead, Christian turned off the engine and stepped out. Martin did the same, after telling us to follow.

"Still think this was a good idea?" I mumbled to Shadia as I pulled my hat from the floor.

"Yes," she answered. "Stay in the car, and I'll come to the other side to support you, OK?"

"Sure," I grumbled, and she undid her belt and climbed out.

Instantly, I saw a ripple go through the people standing on the other side of the fence. Martin was walking that way now, talking as he went.

Shadia opened the car door and gave me a hand. Helping me out, she leaned me against the side of the car and closed the door behind me. I leaned my head against her shoulder, hiding my face from the bright sun.

I could hear Martin say our names, Christian chiming in every now and again. When my eyes had adjusted to the light outside the car, I looked up. Someone was riding a horse deeper into the valley, where I could see a few houses splattered around between fields of yellow and green. On the far side of the valley, only visible because they were built uphill on the foot of the mountain, was a group of houses.

"Now what?" Shadia asked, drawing my attention back to the current situation. Christian and Martin seemed to have finished with the people at the gate and joined us by the car.

"Usually, one of the men would check us out, and we'd get to go home, but seeing as we brought you, we need one of the women to come to check you out. Make sure you aren't hiding any bites," Christian said.

"We told you we aren't bitten," Shadia said, a flash of anger in her voice.

"Sure," Martin said, leaning against the car and fishing a

cigarette out of the pocket on his shirt. "But gotta make sure. Can't be too careful these days."

"I guess not," Shadia answered, then moved to support me a little better. "Can we at least get a chair or something? Standing like this isn't too good for her."

"You can go back into the car if you want. The guards just needed to see you."

Shadia mumbled something not too nice before leaning across me and opening the car door. I slipped inside and sank into the seat, letting out a sigh of relief. My legs had started shaking, and the pain was jumping up and down them like a puppy wanting to play, but with claws and teeth instead of soft paws.

"You OK?" Shadia asked as she slid in beside me, making me lean my head against her shoulder.

"Sure," I answered. "What about you? How do you feel?"

"Tired. Looking forward to a bath and some rest."

"Want me to wash your back?" I asked, but the flirty tone I'd intended didn't make its way into my voice. Shadia chuckled anyway.

"Yes, please."

We sat in silence for a long time before Christian tapped on the door and told us one of the women had arrived to check us out.

I climbed onto Shadia's back, and one of the guards opened a door in the side of the wire-wall and let us into a new building hardly big enough for the three of us. The scent of sawdust hung in the air. The guard hurried out, leaving Shadia and me alone with a woman around fifty years old.

Everything that followed was a quick affair. The woman had us undress to our underwear then looked us over with

254

heavy focus. There was no talking until she was sure we were wound-free, when she introduced herself as Maria, who we would stay with until we moved on.

After the check-up was done, she helped us out of the shed and into the back of a horse-drawn wagon. Once sure we were as comfortable as we could be between the boxes and bags Christian and Martin had brought from the car, she climbed into the driver's seat with the two men, and the wagon jumped forward, soon enough leaving the entrance cage and the five male guards behind.

The car had been removed from the cage and driven to the side, where it stood beneath a shelter of drapes and plastic together with a few other cars.

Turned forward, I saw the valley open up before us. From the car-cage, I had been able to see the houses on the other side of the valley. Now, I saw that we'd been standing on the top of a hill, and as the ground started turning down, I saw the two other farms lying at the bottom of the valley, surrounded by paddocks and gardens filled with trees.

My awe turned to tiredness, however, as the wagon bumped its way down the road. Beside me, Shadia was yawning and doing her best to stay sitting up straight, but I could see in her every move that she was tired.

Maria's home was everything one could expect from a farmhouse. It was small and cramped with a weird floor plan. It would be a nightmare to navigate in a wheelchair, but somehow Shadia managed to get me up the stairs and into the bathroom. There was a huge bathtub there, and all we wanted to do was crawl into it, but before we were allowed, Maria ordered us into the shower.

She had a shower stool from when her mother used to live

there, and I slumped into it and let the hot water stream over me. Actual hot water!

It felt like I had never been clean before. The filth and blood and sweat of the last few weeks melted away, helped by a sponge that I used on the parts I could reach, and Shadia used on my back. Afterwards, I washed her back, but there was nothing sexual in it. We were both too preoccupied with our own bliss at the warm water. When our bodies were clean, we washed our hair with one of a butt-load of shampoos.

Finally, Maria deemed us clean enough to climb into the bathtub. While we were in the shower, she had prepared a bunch of small flasks, and the moment we turned off the spout, she started filling the tub, sprinkling in herbs and oil. A calming scent of lavender and chamomile rose with the steam.

She'd also brought two glasses of watered-down orange juice that stood on a small table beside the tub.

"I would give you wine if we had it–nothing like a hot bath with a glass of wine by your side–but we've banned alcohol here in the valley, for our own protection, so the juice is the best I can do."

When we thanked her, and both assured her that it was fine, she left us to our own devices.

With Shadia's help, I was able to climb into the tub and sink into the steadily rising water. For a second, it felt too hot, like it would melt my skin off, then it became a numb warmth, and I slipped into it with a sigh.

Shadia crawled in opposite me, sneaking her legs to rest beside my hips. I rested my hand on her knee and leaned my head back against the tiled wall. It was cool compared to the heat of the water that now reached to my belly button.

We sat in silence until the water covered our breasts, then

Shadia turned off the spout and sunk a little deeper, resting her head against the edge of the tub. I didn't open my eyes to look at her; I just made lazy circles on her knee with my fingers.

I must have drifted off again, for I had the heavy woolliness of sleep in my head when I woke to the sound of sobbing. The moment I realized what it was, I sat up.

Shadia had pulled away from me, sitting with her knees up to her chin, arms wrapped around her shins and crying, trying to keep quiet so as not to wake me.

"Sha," I murmured, and she hiccupped.

"I'm sorry," she managed between sobs. "I didn't mean to wake you."

"Don't worry about that. What is it?"

"Just ... just everything we've done. André. Drammen. Losing you. I ... we're finally safe." She broke into heart-wrenching sobs again, unable to say another word.

I fumbled about in the water for a second, not sure what to do. Water splashed over the edge of the tub and onto the tiled floor as I pushed past Shadia until she rested her back against my naked chest. The moment I wrapped my arms around her, she gripped them so hard it hurt, but I didn't pull back. Just held her and let her cry. She'd done so much to keep me safe, to get me to this point. Not once had I seen her break. Seen her even consider what she'd done to the zombies that came at us. I guess the bath was just too much.

It took almost an hour before she was all cried out, and I held her all that time. When I thought she would be able to keep it down, I took one of the glasses and handed it to her. It wasn't cold anymore, and the bathwater was tepid, but we didn't care. We both emptied them quickly.

Shadia leaned against me. "I'm sorry," she said again.

I kissed her temple. "Never say sorry for showing your feelings. I'd rather see them than not." She squeezed my hand. "But I need to know, what do you wanna do now?"

"What do you mean?"

"If they'll have us, do you want to stay here? It seems like a safe enough place, and there are people here. We wouldn't be all alone. You wouldn't be alone in taking care of me."

"I don't mind."

"I know you don't, but I'd feel better knowing there were other people around to take care of you when I'm sick."

She didn't answer for the longest time, and I almost started believing she'd fallen asleep before she sighed. "We have to see what they say first. We can't stay if they don't want us."

I squeezed her closer.

We sat in silence a while longer, but the feeling in the room was much lighter now. I could still feel sorrow and fear in the way Shadia clung to me, but it seemed she'd dealt with what she needed to deal with right now and was ready to move forward, wherever that might be. I hoped they would let us stay. I didn't want to take Shadia out there ever again.

Epilogue

Shadia stopped at the bottom of the road and puffed out a breath. It hung in front of her face like a cold mist for a second before the wind pulled it away. Snow flew around her, so thick it almost hid the path, but Max showed the way. The Border Collie was only a few months old, born just before SHTF, and when it came time to find it a home, Kit was more than happy to take it in. The little ankle-biter had been the reason for more than one fight between the wives. It wasn't Kit that had to walk the dog or house train it or anything like that. But seeing how much joy the pup brought her wife made it all worth it for Shadia.

Max came bounding back through the snow, tongue lolling, and his usually black fur spotted with white. He was gangly and full of energy, but Shadia was sure he would sleep well tonight. He loved snow, but it also tired him out like nothing else.

"OK, OK, I'm coming." She huffed and started walking again. The snow reached over her boots and had slipped past her coveralls. She was wet and cold and couldn't wait to get inside to the heat.

The cabin rose out of the snow like a witch's cottage. It was small and new, built just before the snow fell, and just for the three of them. They were Maria's closest neighbor, but still far enough away that the two houses couldn't see each other in this flurry. Maria had planted fruit trees in the garden to give them a feeling of privacy, and they'd made room for a kitchen plot for when spring came. For now, it was all dormant and still, swallowed by the snow.

Shadia hurried up the steps and kicked off the snow from her boots before she crossed the porch. When the weather allowed, they planned to have glass put in around it, so it could work as a greenhouse in winter, as well as a heater. Every little trick to survive the changing seasons and climate of Norway.

Max was at the door, scratching, and the moment it was open enough for him to fit through, he slipped inside. Kit's voice sounded, barely audible over the wind.

Shadia stepped inside and closed the door against the cold. Putting her basket down, she started unfurling her winter clothes. Kit's low laugh came from the bedroom, and Shadia smiled a worried smile to herself.

The cabin only had three rooms. There was a huge room just inside the door that was a combined kitchen and living room to make it easier to heat. They had a generator that fueled the stove and fridge, and when summer came, they would set up solar panels. The old-style cooking stove stood between the living room and the kitchen, its pipe running past the bathroom to keep it somewhat warm, radiating heat to the entire building. A pile of wood almost as high as the ceiling stood beside it. There were a sofa and a shelf with books in the living room, as well as a knitting basket, but that was about it. They didn't need much more.

The bathroom had a small tub, a toilet, and a washing stand. When they could, they tried to not use water, but Maria had been adamant that they could share her water line and should get a hot water generator. It would help Kit, she claimed, and it did. The daily hot baths with oils loosened up her muscles better than anything else, but it tired her out getting from the bedroom to the bathroom, so it was a mixed blessing.

Lifting the basket, Shadia walked through the cabin and into the bedroom. There was a double bed there with room for the two of them and Max, but not much more. A small commode with what clothes they had, and Kit's chair in a corner. It hadn't been used in a while. The curtains were drawn, and there was no light.

"You can light a candle if you want," Kit said, her voice low and weak.

"No need," Shadia said and walked to the bed.

Pushing Max aside, she sat down beside Kit and stroked her cheek. The cheekbone poked at her, hard and prominent.

A week after it became clear they were welcome to stay in Hope Valley–Kit's name, and it stuck with the others who had escaped from the outside world and ended up here–she got sick. Really sick. Worse than Shadia had ever seen her. There was seizure after seizure, and at one point, Shadia and Maria were afraid she would die. Kit couldn't eat, could hardly even drink water. Her own heartbeat could be too loud for her, leaving her in frustrated tears. She slept a lot in those days, thankfully, between the seizures and Shadia trying to coach her to eat.

It was then that Maria said they needed their own place to stay. She would be taking in others that arrived, giving them a temporary home until they moved on or got their own place. But Kit couldn't be moved far, so the leaders agreed to build a cabin for the two women close to Maria, so she could be a safety blanket for Shadia.

As Maria watched over Kit and the men built the cabin and lay the water lines and got the generator set up, Shadia took on the job of teaching the few kids in the valley. Raiding parties brought back schoolbooks and skimming them soon refreshed her memory. She became the local teacher, to the kids' great dismay.

For almost a month and a half, she survived on honeyed milk and a little water a day. She couldn't go to the bathroom, so she had to use a bedpan, which Maria emptied. Moving her hips enough to make room for the pan hurt her, and they were running out of medication fast, even if the raiders looked for it wherever they went. But then Max came, and Kit finally smiled again. The light returned to her eyes, and even as she cried from the pain in her body, she could smile as the pup licked her tears away and tried to make her happy.

"Maria?" Kit asked now.

"She had a new idea for a tea she hoped would help you," Shadia answered.

"Oh."

"You think you're up to trying it?" Kit didn't answer, but her suddenly labored breathing was answer enough. Shadia leaned forward, carefully touching her forehead against Kit's. "Don't think about it, you don't have–"

"Yes," Kit cut her off. "I wanna try, but tomorrow? The weather change wiped me out."

"OK, *habibi*." They sat for a moment. "You need the bathroom?"

"No," Kit answered. "I'm fine."

"OK."

Standing, Shadia moved out of the room and lit a few candles in the kitchen to give her light. Even with the windows out here unobscured by curtains, the snow was drinking up all the sunlight and giving the idea of nightfall even if the sun had barely risen. She put the jar of the new tea on the shelf with Kit's other teas. One for the pain, one for better sleep, one to give her a little energy boost. This new one was supposed to make her want to eat. Shadia hoped it worked. Kit was just skin and bones, and her hair had almost completely fallen out. Even just lifting the duvet was a chore for her.

Shadia leaned her head against the window, feeling the cold of it seep into her skin. But even as bad as Kit was now, she was better than just a few months ago, and she'd been through so much. Her body would take time to deal with everything that had happened, and Shadia's job now was making sure Kit got through it. Making sure she had a chance of enjoying this new life they had found together.

For that was it. They had survived. Outside of Hope Valley, the zombies were as good as gone. People had started making themselves new homes, much like in the Valley, and life went on. But between all of these people, Kit was the only one in a wheelchair that they knew of. She had done the impossible and had the right to take her time getting back on her feet, so to speak. For now, she was alive, and in a few months, or a few years, she could actually live.

"Sha?" Kit's voice was weak but still carried in the small, quiet cabin.

"Yes?" Shadia asked, pushing away from the window and leaning through the doorway.

She could just make out the small shape of Kit under the duvet in the candlelight, Max lying with his head on her hip, soaking the fabric with melting snow and not caring. Kit's thin, pale hand was buried in his fur, stark against his blackness.

"Do you think we could try reading a little more today?"

Shadia couldn't help the smile that pulled at her lips. "Of course, *habibi*. In bed?"

"Yeah."

Without a word, Shadia walked into the living room and found the book she was reading aloud for her wife. Lighting one of the oil lamps they'd been given, she blew out the candles and walked into the bedroom. Kit had covered her eyes with her mask, but she was smiling.

Shadia hung the lamp on its hook on the wall and climbed into her side of the bed. Pushing away Max, Kit carefully and slowly turned around until she lay facing Shadia, resting one hand on her thigh. The hand was shaking minutely, but it was still a touch. Opening the book, Shadia began to read, a smile on her lips.

They had survived, they were still alive, and no matter how much time it might take, they would live together again.

The End

Acknowledgment

I have many a soul to thank for getting Survival Kit to the stage it is today.

The first one is my husband, Sven, for standing by my side through my own sickness, and as I wrote this book. It was an extreme emotional toil writing something this personal, and he was there for me every step of the way.

Some thanks must also be given to the M.E.-community in Norway. They gave me a place to air my grief as well as friends to lean on. They made me feel less alone in an impossible situation and have helped me live with it thus far.

Regarding the actual writing of this book, the first person who needs thanks is my good friend Joakim. He helped me on the science-front of the zombies. His knowledge has been a blessing!

I must also thank my fantastic beta readers: Øystein, Patrik, Niels, Kima, Beate, and Zack. Your feedback was invaluable.

Thank you to Vicky, my editor, for doing such a good job.

And thank you so, so much to Ravven for making this amazing cover!

Finally, thank you, reader, for picking up this book.

About the Author

Anniken Haga published her first novel in Norwegian in 2014. This was an NA thriller set in her hometown. In 2015 and 2016, she published two MG fantasy books, also in Norwegian.
They were all published through Liv Forlag.

Deciding to go Indie, she published her first English work-Artificial Generation-in 2018.

You can connect with me on:
🐦 https://twitter.com/AnnikenHaga
f https://www.facebook.com/hagaanniken

Subscribe to my newsletter:
✉ https://landing.mailerlite.com/webforms/landing/h6a0b5

Also by A. H. Haga

Artificial Generation
Elena is part of a generation of artificially created children.Believed to be humankind's last hope, they have only one purpose: to breed.Elena, however, doesn't want children.

If she goes against the Council, she risks losing everything she ever cared about.

When her world is attacked, threatening to end their very way of life, Elena must fight for her, and her peers', right to live how they want and make their own choices.

Printed in Great Britain
by Amazon